The Devil Is a
Black Dog

Stories from
the Middle East and Beyond

The Devil Is a Black Dog

Stories from the Middle East and Beyond

Sándor Jászberényi

Translated from the Hungarian
by M. Henderson Ellis

New Europe Books

Williamstown, Massachusetts

Contents

To Hafiz

The Fever

I'm sick. My temple throbs. I can feel my entire nervous system, down to every last nerve ending. My head is wrung out. It hurts. My mouth is like dry clay, as if I haven't had water for days. Just a few minutes ago I was gazing listlessly at the rocky desert as it flew past. Now, if I turn my head, the landscape comes with me. It slips, like the sound in an old video recording. I don't know where I caught this sickness. Perhaps when we crossed Lake Nasser. We had to hurry on the Egyptian side and scrambled to get tickets for the ferry. I remember how thirsty I was in the market, and that I drank from a communal clay pot. Yes, perhaps it was the water, the green water of the lake.

It is also possible that I became infected in Abuja. I was staying in a damp room in a boarding house called the Hotel Mechko. I didn't think twice that there was no mosquito netting on the windows or bed. Hundreds of bugs must have sucked my blood that night while the rainy season bellowed outside.

Or perhaps it found me in the air of Kinshasa, Mombasa, or Aden. Or came from the roaches that crawled across me at night in hotel rooms, or from holding hands or a lover's embrace; for everything is infectious in the tropics. If you live here, you know you can't avoid disease. Even with an iron constitution, the continent will get a taste of you sooner or later. Of course there is preventative medicine, but the side effects are so strong that it is not out of irresponsibility that you decline them. Who would want to bear the continual retching and nausea in 110-degree heat, when the bottom of your mouth is dry as paper and your lungs are burning with such hot, steamy air that you think you are breathing fire?

No, living in the tropics isn't about overcoming disease but trying to survive it. You should be ready, because it is unavoidable. And vaccinations are useless. I remember how proudly I asserted to a doctor while walking between beds of the slumbering TB patients in the leper and tuberculosis hospital in Zaria, Nigeria, that I was inoculated and thus didn't need a face mask.

"There are no vaccinations for this," responded the doctor. He explained that TB patients are put to sleep in the last stages of their disease so they don't suffocate while awake.

Most African diseases come with fever. When it begins, time pauses. The hand on the wristwatch doesn't move, the wind doesn't blow sand. There is nothing to a person, just a body. One that is about to betray you.

The woman I'm traveling with, Zeinab's her name, comes from the Fur tribe. I pay five dollars a day for her love. We have a special ritual for the payment. In the morning, after we make love, she gets her backpack, takes out her leather wallet, stands in front of me, and says, "A new day is beginning, so pay." I pay. Her teeth flash in the morning light as she smiles. We've been together for two months. I think she's in love with me, and I probably haven't needed to give her any money for a while now, but I do anyway, so she can't use that against me when it ends.

"You'll take me home with you, right? So I can see the snow."

"I'll take you."

"You were joking, right? When you said you have no soul."

"I was joking."

"Because if you don't have a soul, how can you go to heaven or hell?"

"What makes you think I want to go anywhere?"

"Because you are always traveling."

"And?"

"There is nothing wrong with travel, that's not why I said it. I love traveling with you. Traveling, making love, drinking beer, and eating opium for nice dreams."

When Zeinab sees I am in trouble, she tells the driver. His name is Abdul Sabur, and he drives barefoot. I had contracted him in Khartoum to take me to Sawakin, because I wanted to see the face of evil. Zeinab told me it's a haunted place, where the devil sits on your chest at night.

Along with that, there was also a civil war, and the tribes were on the move; this is what I am supposed to write about. We're traveling in a thirty-year-old black Ford Cortina. My woman turns toward me and says something, but I can't make sense of her words, which come to me in gurgling sounds. She presses a plastic bottle of water into my hand. I lift it to my mouth and drink. The water should be warm, but it feels cold to me, and makes my esophagus ache. I see Zeinab's expression of worry, tears forming in her eyes as she begins to recite the Koran. In Africa, when there is trouble, everybody turns devout. For example, once during a police raid on a Cairo brothel, I saw a Saudi man, who wasn't in the least bit religious, swear on the Koran that he was only there by accident.

Abdul Sabur turns toward me. He looks terrified. I don't under-stand why, until I see my face in the rearview mirror. My eyes are blood red and my pupils have all but disappeared. Abdul pulls off the main road and heads in the direction of a village. Mud huts appear against a horizon of beaten red earth and goats. The inhabitants stand at the huts' entrances and stare at us as we come to a stop in the village commons.

"It'll be alright," says Zeinab. I respond in Hungarian. When a fever is up around 107 degrees you forget all languages but your own.

Abdul Sabur opens the door and I try to get out. All my muscles stiffen and tense, and I can't bend my leg. Tears of pain flow from the effort, and in the end I fall flat on my face. I taste salt in my mouth; perhaps it's blood. Men from the town rush to-ward us; they lift me up and carry me into one of the huts. Inside it's dim, and smells of smoke and feces. They lay me by the fire.

"Halfan," I say. "I have Malaria, bring Halfan." A black man with tattoos on his face says that the nearest pharmacy is in a city ninety miles away.

Abdul Sabur departs immediately, but on this road he won't get back until dawn, which means a twelve-hour wait. Zeinab col-lapses in tears. She knows that in twelve hours death could come knocking a thousand times. More, if the person is a foreigner.

Crying suits her. The straps of her blouse fall down and I can see her shoulders. It reminds me of how, on our first days together—when she only wanted to make love—she would sleep only on her back. She paid careful attention, on the soiled bed, under the fan, to be sure I wouldn't see her body, having wrapped herself in a blanket. Then, once after I followed her into the shower, I figured out what she was hiding: the bloody scars given to her by her father; the same man who had molested her and finally went blind from the Nile water and 80-proof moonshine made with embalming fluid.

The village women bring clay pots of water into the hut. Zeinab takes the scarf from her neck, dampens it, and wipes my brow. I plead with her to stop, because it hurts. I feel like I am floating a yard above the ground. From an opening cut in the ceiling I can see the violet-blue, cloudless sky. My eyes get used to the blue. A Hungarian song plays in my mind, and I may even be singing loudly along. The old woman sitting next to me chews betel, her spit forming red pools on the ground. She holds my head up for ten minutes or so as she feeds me on goat milk. I take it without protest; I don't even have the strength to gag. After that, I don't know how much time passes. Finally the door opens and Zeinab steps in, accompanied by a man in a long beard, wearing a jellabiya, holding a Koran in his hand.

In Sudan every village has at least one sheikh and one *faki*. While the sheikh relies on the Koran and white magic to heal, the faki's power comes from the dirty little deals he strikes with the devil. In Khartoum, for example, for twenty dollars I bought an amulet that, when stitched into my clothing, was supposed to protect me from bullets. There was one for sickness as well. I should have bought that one.

"But he isn't a Muslim," says the sheikh, turning toward my woman. In response she takes a five-dollar bill from her wallet, puts it in his hand, and says, "Just try."

He kneels over me. With the Koran stuck under my arm, the sheikh begins to recite an incantation against demonic possession. It doesn't help. If the devil is inside of me, he has lived there for a long time. He's dug himself in, and won't be roused by any common village exorcist.

I turn on my side and can see my father standing there. He is in his brown jacket, a collar shirt, and is looking down at me with a strict, professorial expression.

"The increasing body temperature bolsters the immune system in the many segments of the spine while also stemming the spread of pathogenic bacteria," he says and nods, to which I say, "That's for sure, Dad."

"This is what you wanted, right? Do you at least know what you are looking for here?" he asks.

"I'm a correspondent. It's my job to go to places like this."

I smile, because I know this is not the whole truth, but I won't tell that to my father, especially if he happens to be the product of a fever-induced dream.

He disappears, but I can't stop smiling. The sheikh completes his recitation from the Koran; and again Zeinab collapses in tears. In Darfur, where she comes from, if a patient begins to smile, it means he or she is about to die. Around there peaceful deaths are few, but held in great esteem.

But that is not why I am smiling. I am smiling because I don't regret anything, really. I never wanted to live a sensible life. I didn't want to be a model citizen; I desired neither a family nor children, and when I found myself in possession of both, the enterprise wound up a dismal failure. I have answers only when the circumstances are clear, like life and death; that's when I feel best, when the questions are easy, uncomplicated by the reflexes of a dying civilization.

I lift my head, so I can establish that I have indeed lost my sight. Everything looks white, blinding white, as though I am staring into the sun. The world goes quiet as my life begins to flash before my eyes. I am not afraid. I didn't want a sensible death either.

Professional Killers

We were lying among the trees in the yard. The sweet smell of fruit was everywhere. Bees and wasps buzzed above our heads. The sun shone through the leaves and warmed us through our clothing; it was a good feeling. We liked being there, in the garden behind the house, where nobody had a word to say to us. It was just my little brother and I on that early afternoon.

We lay there silently plucking the fallen sour cherries from the grass, eating the soft flesh and making a game of shooting the wet pits from between our fingers. It was then that my brother noticed the bird. He poked me in the shoulder and pointed to a cherry tree. I followed the line indicated by his finger to the lowest branch, where the crow was perched. It was a big one, the branch dipping under its weight.

Until then we had seen its kind only in the plowed fields around our village; they never came so close as to venture into the trees on our property. We had tried to see one from up close before, but unlike smaller birds, these were too intelligent and cunning to let us near.

I felt my pulse quicken, and I reached over to grab our gun, a Slovak-made air rifle. Its black oily barrel flashed in the sunlight as I pulled it close. Dad had tricked it out with a tighter spring, so that we could hunt with it. We were so proud of that rifle—a firearm of our own. We didn't mind sharing it; we shared everything else.

I sat up and cracked the barrel. I dug some ammo from my pocket, trying to make sure none of the excess rounds fell out. We had only 923 pellets for the entire summer, as many as came in one box. Dad said he wouldn't buy us more, so we would have to take care of how we used them. We had done the math and figured we could shoot no more than ten rounds a day, but after Father stopped supervising us, the ration was soon forgotten.

I loaded the gun. With my thumb, I gently pushed in the lead pellet and cracked the barrel back in place. I momentarily worried that the sound had startled the crow. I froze, sitting dead still. But the bird wasn't concerned with us. It was much more interested in the fruit dangling off the tree's outer branches. It preened itself, and lazily plucked the nearby cherries with its beak.

I carefully rested the rifle against my shoulder, looked into the sight, and tried to control my breath. My brother began to squirm beside me.

"Sure you can hit it from here?" he whispered.

"Yep."

"We already used one pellet today."

"Well, this guy is worth at least two notches."

With a pocketknife we had been carving notches into the gun after every kill, just like the American Indians had done in our books about them. We had sworn that by summer's end there would be fifty notches cut into in the gun's stock. Though a month and a half had already passed, we had only accumulated eighteen. My brother didn't think we would make it; for

his part, he was too small to properly hold the gun, and this
resulted in lots of misfires. As for me, I wasn't too worried
about it: from the moment I picked up that rifle I was a professional killer.

When he gave us the weapon, our father instructed us to make
only clean kills. Figuring that sooner or later we would realize that
rifles weren't invented for mere target practice, he reasoned that it
would be better if he told us all we had to know.

We were standing in the yard, and the smell of potatoes
stewed in paprika sauce wafted through the air. Then, right before
our eyes, our father shot a sparrow from its perch on the branch
of a walnut tree. "One shot, one kill," he said. One shot: that's
what he meant by "clean." He went on to explain that if we killed
something (as he was sure we would), we shouldn't play with the
dead body afterward. If we kill, we should do it quickly and precisely. Anything that has a heart must be shown respect.

In the first few weeks, we actually weren't able to shoot a
thing, but not long afterward we got the hang of it. We soon
became drunk on the power, knowing we could have this impact;
where before there was this living, moving creature, now there
was nothing but carrion on the ground. We had killed ants and
other bugs before, but this sort of daring was a new and seductive
feeling. We'd proudly pick up the shot sparrows by their feet, and
bring them to the graves we had already dug for them. He who
had made the kill completed the ritual: carving our mark into the
stock of the rifle.

"I'm hungry," my brother said, sitting up.

"Eat some cherries," I replied, without turning to look at
him.

"I'm sick of cherries."

"We'll eat after this shot. Dad's coming home soon."

I flattened myself on the ground. I didn't want to startle the bird. I looked at my watch. Dad was indeed a bit late for lunch, and I was also hungry.

Our mother had been in the hospital since the beginning of the summer. Dad was almost certainly with her now. Since it had become apparent that there was something wrong with her womb, that she had to be admitted to the hospital, Dad didn't do much but shuttle between my mother's bedside, work, and home. My brother and I didn't know exactly what Mom was sick with, as they had taken care to talk about it only after they put us to bed.

I remember that on the day before she went to the hospital, I found Dad crying in the kitchen. He said everything would be alright. Then they left for the hospital and he didn't return for days. For two months he spent all his time there. It became normal for my brother and I to cry ourselves to sleep, though we eventually gave this up, as we became distracted by the impending summer.

Dad wouldn't let us come with him on visits. He said that we were still too young for this. We communicated with Mom by drawing her pictures and writing her letters. I was in second grade and could already write well. I composed serious letters to her, filled with sentences like, "Today we hunted in the woods." My brother mainly sent crayon-drawn pictures of volcanoes, tanks, or whatever happened to be on his mind that day.

Since our mother's disappearance, there were lots of changes at home. For instance, Dad didn't play with us anymore. He became irritable, lost a lot of weight, and took up smoking again.

"Can I try?" asked my brother.

"No."

"But you got the last turn."

"That's because you still can't shoot so well," I said, lowering the gun.

"It's not fair that you always get to shoot."

"You still can't load it properly without my help."

"But it's still not fair that you always get to shoot!"

"You can go next, OK?"

I whispered that last sentence because I noticed the crow begin to stir. Then, with languid flaps of its wings, it flew from the cherry tree to the top branch of a pine that stood by the house. We jumped up and raced in that direction, keeping an eye out to find the best position to fire from. We didn't bicker anymore after that.

I took a place by our green, rusty fence, and again raised the rifle to my shoulder. I shifted my aim a few centimeters left and calculated the path of the bullet. I felt a slight breeze against my face. Though it wouldn't be strong enough to push the bullet off its path, I still wanted to be sure, so I concentrated on guessing the exact trajectory. I pressed the rifle butt into my shoulder and left it there, allowing my grip to become more relaxed so I could release the pellet more easily, just like Dad had taught me.

The shooter needs to fire after exhaling, because when you breathe in, your shoulders move. With the sight, I found the crow, and aimed at its neck. I waited for the right moment, when I could no longer feel the weight of the rifle in my hands.

The lead pellet's report echoed through the air. The bird fell from the tree as I, with a triumphant smile, lowered the rifle from my shoulder. We rushed over to where the crow had fallen. It was still alive, though my shot had hit it in the neck. It flapped spasmodically about on the path in front of us, trying to take flight. We watched it in its death throes from a few steps away. We had never seen anything like it.

I reloaded the gun, took aim at the bird's breast, and fired. Feathers flew from its body where the pellet entered. It tried to stand, but was unable. Blood from its wounds spread across the cement sidewalk.

"Die already!" my brother shouted. I searched my pocket for another pellet and loaded the rifle again.

This time I found the crow's wing, the force of the shot propelling the bird onto its feet. Now standing, it ceased beating its wings. After a moment it noticed us and began to hobble our way, dragging its limp wings behind it, the wound in its neck dripping blood down the feathers of its breast. I reloaded, and shot.

I hit it in its chest, but that didn't stop it. I began to retreat, because I was afraid its blood would get on me. The crow was perhaps a yard from me when it lifted its head and looked right at me, its eyes black as buttons.

It began to caw, unbearably loud, and without pause. I shot it again, but it was as if the crow didn't even notice.

"It doesn't want to die!" my brother cried, in hysterics now. "You can't kill it," he shrieked, and ran away.

The crow continued to come for me; I tried to reload, but after I had emptied my pocket, I was left with an empty gun.

When it was right in front of me, it stopped and again resumed its piercing cry. It was so close I could see its tongue moving in its beak. The gun fell from my hands and clattered on the ground. Blood pounded in my temple and my sweat turned cold. With nowhere else to go, I pressed my entire body against the fence, so hard that the chain links would leave their impression on my back. I couldn't kill the bird. Our eyes locked, and we stared each other down. As I gazed into the bird's black eyes, my tears began to flow.

"What in God's name are you doing?"

It was Dad. He stood by the fence, cigarette in hand.

In one swift motion he was beside me. He gave the bird a swift kick, and I heard the crow's bones break. The kick sent the bird flying into the air, black feathers falling in its wake. It met with the wall of the house, leaving a bloody stain where it hit.

Still, it wasn't dead. It cried pitifully and bled on the ground, again trying to stand. My father picked up the air rifle, stepped over to the bird, and with all his strength, smashed the crow's head with the butt of the gun. He had to hit it several times until he finally cracked open its skull. I couldn't move; I just stood there and watched as fluff from the animal's feathers flew into the air. It was all over in a few seconds, after which he used some grass to wipe the blood from the rifle.

That night, I came down with a fever. I tossed and turned in my bed and kicked the blanket from my body. If I closed my eyes, the crow appeared, coming for me, a wholly unkillable beast coming for me. I whimpered loud enough to bring Dad into my room. It was already late at night, but he was still in his street clothes. He sat on the side of my bed and stroked my forehead, then stuck a thermometer under my arm. I could smell cigarettes and beer on his breath.

"I don't know how I messed up," I said to him, my voice trembling. "I did everything you taught me, but I couldn't kill the thing the right way."

"You didn't do anything bad. Not even God can make a clean kill all the time," he said. He patted me on my head, then tucked me in again before going back to his room and turning up the music.

The Blake Precept

I was in Abéché, Chad. I was supposed to fly to N'Djamena, but two days before my departure the Haboob descended. It came savagely from above Darfur, and under the orders of the UN all flights were cancelled for safety reasons. The locals knew it was coming; their camels wouldn't drink, instead they just stamped their hooves restlessly and shook themselves loose from their ropes. One camel kicked a boy in the chest who had dared to get too close, breaking four ribs. Within moments, the streets were empty of people.

I was at the airport, ready to go, when the news was broadcast. "Don't be too distressed," said the pilot, who was standing next to me. He informed me that within spitting distance was a Legion base, and that its commanding officer was quite an affable guy. I could probably pass the night there while the storm calmed, and I might even get something to drink in the canteen. With nothing else to do, I gathered myself and started walking toward the base, which was perhaps two kilometers from the airport. As I went, the sky covered over, and the wind began to blow with terrifying strength. Soon the clouds were so full of dust it seemed like it was night, though it was still early afternoon.

Then came the sand. It burned when it hit, and there was no keeping it from getting in my boots and under my clothing, where it scoured my skin into blood-red scrapes. It took a concerted effort just to make my way down the short road, as I continually had to stop and wipe grains from my eyes and clean them from my ears. By the time I arrived at the Legion's double-gated, modern fortress, I was virtually blind. The man on guard pointed his gun at me and began shouting. He left his post to better see who I was. It wasn't an easy job, because the storm was raging ever stronger, and every exposed part of me was painted by sand: I could have been anybody. When he realized I wasn't a local, he let me in, directing me toward the building marked by the words "Nihil Obstat." There I would find the canteen, and in it I would find the commander of the base. And so I went.

In the canteen sat a man dressed in typical combat fatigues, gaping at the storm through the window. He greeted me, and I introduced myself and explained my predicament. He was indeed a nice person, and French; Jules Lacroix was his name. He was the commander, and the highest ranking of the four hundred or so legionnaires stationed there. Without asking, he put food in front of me and brought a bowl of water, so I could wash the sand from my face and hands. He immediately proposed that I stay in the camp for as long as the Haboob held us in its grips. He would arrange everything, on the condition that I attend an evening poker party with the officers. I saw no reason why not, and we laughed and shook hands on the deal. He then invited me to his quarters, where he offered me whisky and beer. We drank four beers each, and only then did I begin to relax. Outside the storm wailed with full force.

We talked about Africa, Europe, and anything that came to mind. He was pleased to have my company, as he rarely saw

Europeans in these parts, especially those who weren't on the run from the law, though these types were mostly already serving under him. For six years, he hadn't set foot outside of Africa. He was a generous sort, and listened attentively when I told of my own travels. He spoke mostly of the difficulty in living there, the unit's losses, the tropical sickness, and how Africa was like a huge branding iron, leaving its stamp on anybody who happened to find their way to near the equator. . . . A knock came at the door, and a young conscript entered.

"Commander, ten of the men would like to go into town for some R and R," he said and clicked his heels. The commander momentarily looked over the soldier, and then assented with a wave of his hand. I watched on, dumbfounded. I couldn't imagine that anybody would want to be out in this storm. Before the conscript left the room, Lacroix called after him, "Remind them that the Blake Precept is in effect!" Noting my expression, he leaned back in his chair, lit a cigarette, and reminded me that this was the French Foreign Legion. His men could eat this little storm for breakfast. "But much more interesting is the Blake Precept," he said, and poured us both another whisky. He lifted his glass and said, "Let's drink to the Blake Precept." We drank. Then he told the story of Sam Blake.

Blake was an Australian captain who was in the Legion about five years ago. Blake wasn't alive anymore, but he had received a posthumous Croix de le Valeur Militaire, the highest level of state and military decoration. His story went like this. He had been transferred into the Chad armed corps as a driver. During that time, the Darfur conflict was raging, and six tribes from three countries were killing each other for the region's arable land. The frontiers were totally unstable, which is why the Legion had been deployed there.

Blake was a relaxed, quiet man. There was nothing to really distinguish him from the other soldiers; he was neither braver nor more cowardly, exactly as a true legionnaire should be. On weekends he went into town with the others. There is not much to do in an outback dustbowl like Abéché, though there was a bar and a whorehouse. It was on one such weekend when it happened. He was drinking with a fellow officer in the bar of the town's only hotel, when one of their translators showed up at the door and asked if they wanted to see something they would likely never find anywhere else in the world. Blake and his friend weren't especially thirsty, so they agreed. They followed the translator, who took them to a ghost rider.

The Darfur conflict had mixed everything up and triggered a movement of the tribes. Along with the upheaval a lot of strange phenomena emerged. The ghost riders were one of them. These were locals capable of letting a ghost possess their bodies and speak with their tongue. The tribes greatly respected these people. They heaped offerings on them, and consulted them with their lives' gravest questions.

It was already late when Blake's group arrived at the ghost rider's hut on the edge of town. The ghost rider was an old Kununbu man, and the fingers of his left hand were missing, though it was still possible to count on the five stumps. According to the translator, he would be visited by the spirit of a great Sudanese warlord when he clutched a white-hot ember in his hands. The two legionnaires sat on the floor of the hut and handed over gifts (scarcely worth a dollar) then waited for the old man to perform. The ghost rider smiled at them, flashing a mouth of missing teeth, then without the slightest indication of pain, put his left hand into the fire and scooped out an ember. The irises of his eyes turned white, and he spoke in a greatly altered voice.

"You are allowed one question," said the translator. "Just one question each."

Blake smirked and asked, "How will I die?"

"It won't be by bullet," said the aged man. "But you will die when you rise into the air like a bird."

Neither of them thought much of it: Europeans hadn't believed in things like this since the French Enlightenment, though it transpired that Blake would indeed never be hit by a bullet. That very week he was sent in a convoy to Goz Beïda, a place where it was possible to see low-flying Sudanese bombers dropping ignited barrels of gasoline over villages. On the streets eight different armies were mixing, looting anything they could. The border was mined, to be certain the tribes wouldn't cross. Blake and perhaps thirty other people were delivering medicine to the refugee camp when they were ambushed. It wasn't an amateur piece of work: they were lit up with sprays of gunfire from atop four hills, while RPGs on the ground took out the vehicles. Everyone died with the exception of Blake, who fled across the minefield and returned fire from the far side. When it was all over, he hadn't suffered a scratch.

When he returned to the camp, he was called a hero and immediately promoted. The other legionnaires embraced him, patted him on the back, and said he was born under a lucky star, and that's why he didn't take a bullet. But Blake wouldn't talk about the incident and whenever anybody asked, he just began to hum. Everybody knew you couldn't survive something like this without divine intervention. After that, the commander tried to give him less dangerous assignments, but Blake only volunteered for riskier and riskier missions. And he returned from each one. As his brothers-in-arms fell, he remained unscratched, fearless even in the fiercest hail of bullets. News of his heroics spread, and he was promoted to captain. Blake was up for anything aside from flying in a plane. This was the one thing nobody could persuade him to do.

The news of Blake soon reached the Legion's top brass. The story pleased one of the generals, and he decided that the time had come to give a commendation to the young officer. He telegrammed his decision to the camp commander, who then read the decree out loud in front of the whole detachment. When the news broke among the soldiers, they took the hero on their shoulders. Blake was the only one who wasn't celebrating. The commendation, he learned, would be handed out in Paris. And he would have to fly there. As the time for the ceremony approached, Blake became increasingly nervous; he fought and spoke disrespectfully to his superiors, so that they would demote him and he would be passed over for the medal. His superiors, however, just thought it was the pressure showing, and let the digressions go, even overlooking it when he returned from leave terribly drunk with two prostitutes.

The day arrived when he was to fly to Paris. The Legion had sent a private plane especially for the occasion, with two generals aboard to escort him. Blake, however, wouldn't leave the barracks. He shouted out that he would shoot anybody who tried to put him on the plane, and didn't they know that the ghost rider said he would die if he flew? The military police had to put him in shackles and drag him to the plane as he whimpered between them like a child. The entire company saw it and heard what he said, and thought the poor guy had gone crazy.

The plane never arrived in Paris. Due to a technical problem the pilot had to make an emergency landing before even reaching the Chad border. The plane exploded on impact. There were no survivors. As talk of this episode got around, more and more soldiers began to visit the ghost riders. It got so bad that some soldiers gave up showering, shaving, wearing the Kepi Blanc, and one wouldn't even ride in a car, heeding what a ghost rider had forewarned. The camp commander instituted a penalty to get them back in line. This is how the Blake Precept was born. If any legionnaire was caught consulting a ghost rider, he would be locked away for four weeks in solitary confinement, and in Africa it averages 105 degrees, so it's nobody's idea of fun. . . .

After the commander finished the story, we continued drinking, then later went to play poker in the canteen. I was lucky, winning almost a hundred bucks. The storm raged on into the night, so they showed me to a bed. I slept very well. The morning was bright, clear, and beautiful; the Haboob had blown back to Sudan. The commander insisted on having breakfast with me before I left. At the canteen, the Blake Precept was still on my mind. Now there was almost nobody at the camp who would have known Blake personally, outside of the commander and a repairman from barrack number three. I couldn't stand it any longer, so I asked the commander how well he knew Blake. "I was with him in the ghost rider's hut," he said, and stopped eating. He looked me in the eye. "Don't worry, everything will be OK for me, so long as Lake Chad doesn't dry up."

I made my flight to N'Djamena, and from there I traveled on to Tripoli and then Cairo. In my hurry, I forgot all about Commander Lacroix. I arrived in Cairo and threw myself into my work. Four months later, on a Cairo-to-Budapest flight, the commander popped into my mind, when, after the meal, I opened the in-flight magazine. There was a longish article about how Lake Chad was drying up at an astounding rate, and now it didn't even reach Nigeria. A brief shudder ran through me as I recalled the prophecy of the ghost rider. Later that spring it wasn't totally unexpected news that the rebels had attacked and taken Abéché. There were no survivors.

How Ahmed Salem Abandoned God

When Mubarak stepped down, the cafés reopened. I thought this would be a good time to go for a few glasses of beer and wash away the taste of tear gas. I got in a cab and told the driver to take me to the Horreya Café, at the end of the Corniche, on Falaki Square.

The wind from the open window ruffled my shirt. The Nile was red with the desert's piercing sun. Boats bobbed in the water, their lights out.

A sand-colored Abrams tank stood at the intersection, slowing traffic, the barrel pointing toward the city center. At the gun turret slouched a mustached soldier. A younger conscript was checking the papers of the people in our lane, his AK-47 clattering against his shoulder when he leaned into the open windows. His fatigues were colored brown with patches of sweat.

"Good evening," he said, and had a look at my passport. He indicated that we could carry on. The taxi driver and I exchanged glances.

"It's freedom," the man said with a smile. He was used to the police taking foreigners from his car.

"Let's not celebrate just yet."

We continued on, taking the long way around Tahrir Square, which was closed off by the military. At Saad Zaghloul Square I decided to get out and walk a bit. There were hardly any people on the streets. Shards of broken glass grated under my sandals, and smoke still rose from the smoldering trash cans that had been used as barricades. It felt good to walk in the city center, with nobody out to kill me. I had covered the whole revolution. After a few days I got used to the tear gas, but not the explosions from the Molotov cocktails or the sound of machine-gun fire. On the other hand, I had become accustomed to living without my usual comforts. Alcohol was the first to go, then I quit smoking, and then as the situation got worse, hot showers, and finally bedding. It's entirely possible to sleep well on potato sacks, among rats, if you happen to find yourself in a produce market, hiding from a bloodthirsty mob that wants your neck.

Biled, the alcoholic Coptic headwaiter, was standing outside the Horreya, smoking. I took a long drag from my own cigarette, ground the butt into the side of my sandal, then kicked it into the street.

"I thought they would have arrested you by now," he said with a smile once he noticed me.

"They did. Three times."

"Then what are you doing here?"

"They let me go."

"Well, that's a different story. Go on, take a seat in the back."

We shook hands, and I made my way to the rear of the café, which was cordoned off. Biled didn't like the beer drinkers to sit by the window, lest it provoke the devout Muslims outside. He sent everybody to the back if the place wasn't full, or if he had yet to drink enough not to care. I sat down. Without asking, he put an Egyptian Stella in front of me. The beer was cold, the foam bubbling over the rim and flowing down the bottle in a thin stream, wetting my fingers. I lifted it to my lips and took a long swig. I savored the sensation of the bubbly liquid flooding the back of my mouth until the smell of malt rose into my nose. I felt like a new man.

After I finished the beer, I looked around the café, hoping to spot somebody I knew. It is not good to drink alone. I didn't count on finding a foreigner; most had left the country at the first sign of trouble, and the Western journalists would all be drinking at flashy places like the Hilton Ramses or the Estoril, where it's possible to buy foreign-made beer. A few of the usual gay boys sat at the tables draped with fly-shit covered plastic tablecloths, and a group of shorthaired Sudanese hookers were trawling for customers. I called over to Biled to bring me another beer. Somebody at the bar had left behind the day's issue of *Al-Ahram*. The front page lauded the victims of the revolution. The martyrs' faces were emblazoned in miniature hand-drawn portraits. The headline printed in red announced, "840 DEAD IN THREE WEEKS." Underneath it the subheading read, "THE NUMBER OF WOUNDED STANDS ABOVE 6,000."

I looked up when a new customer entered and watched a man of around sixty sit down at a table near me. He was dressed in a white jellabiya and a white traditional hat, and he wore a beard that was cut and dyed according to the Sunnah dictates. His forehead was darkened by the callus that adorned the devout, who prayed with their heads to the rug five times a day.

"What can I bring you, Doctor?" asked Biled.

"A Stella."

The headwaiter placed a beer in front of the man, who immediately slugged it down.

"Another."

"As you wish, Doctor."

I sat by, astounded. You rarely meet an alcoholic Islamist in Cairo. Biled picked up on my surprise, stepped over to my table, and intoned quietly in my ear, "Don't bother Ahmed Salem. I'll explain the whole thing later."

I returned to my beer and continued to look over the paper. The Islamist stared ahead of himself and drank mechanically. In under half an hour, seven empty bottles of Stella sat before him. My head awash in beer, I lost myself again in the paper. It was highly entertaining to read about how the military and the people were friends, and of the impending democratic reforms, and the celebration of "our new heroes." I then noticed that somebody was standing next to my table. It was one of the Sudanese prostitutes. She wore a flower-patterned dress, and stood with her hands on her hips, flashing a perfect row-full of white teeth.

"I know what you're here for," she said, and licked her lips. "Buy me a beer?"

I put on my glasses to better take her in. Her nipples poked out through her dress, as she had probably pinched them into shape before coming over. She had a beautiful body, young and strong. An image of her naked flesh flashed through my mind: her brown breasts, her totally black nipples. I hadn't been with a woman in a month, yet still I shook my head no. I had spent too much money already in recent weeks to be able to afford the company. Her smile melted away and she clicked her tongue at me scornfully before heading off to the washroom. The Islamist had just finished his ninth beer. When the woman passed his table, he reached out his hand to stop her. He whispered something I couldn't hear, then the man stood up and reached into the pocket of his jellabiya, pulled out a 100-pound note, and dropped it on the table. The girl and the older man staggered arm in arm toward the exit. They made a striking, inexplicable pair.

"Good-bye, Doctor," called Biled before they disappeared into the night. I looked after their shapes as they faded away down the block.

It was approaching curfew, and most of the customers had already left. Only us two were left as the fridge rumbled and the ceiling fans churned about the night air. With one of his filthy rags, Biled swatted a fly, then grabbed a glass, sat next to me, and helped himself to my beer.

"The revolution has brought out something different in everybody," he said. "The man you just saw, well, he abandoned God." Biled's face reflected neither sadness nor triumph: he was simply establishing the facts. The beer washed the dirt from the edge of his glass as he tipped it back.

"Is he a friend of yours?" I asked.

"He is called Ahmed Salem."

"Is he in the Muslim Brotherhood?"

"No, he had nothing to do with politics."

"He wore the traditional dress of those in the Brotherhood."

"I don't think he had time to change. It is also possible he doesn't have any other clothing."

He took a cigarette from my pack, put it in his mouth, and looked for a lighter in his pocket. When he didn't find one, he took my butane lighter from the table and lit up.

"How well do you know him?" I asked, also taking a cigarette.

"He is my neighbor on Qasr al-Ayni Street. He's a doctor. I used to go to him for this and that."

"How do you know he gave up God?"

"Invite me for a beer and I will tell you."

Biled had a terrible habit of mooching from customers' drinks, smoking their cigarettes, or simply inviting himself to sit down. His position as headwaiter, however, could mean life or death to a guy like me, so it wasn't wise to point fingers. I nodded.

He stood, went to retrieve two beers from the fridge, returned, and placed the drinks on the table.

"Here's how it is. Salem was a good Muslim, and deeply religious. He had an unshakable belief that God was everywhere, and he totally submitted himself to his religion."

"I always envy optimists," I said dryly.

"Me too." Biled took a long swig from his drink. "In any case, he kept his faith even when there was reason to doubt. For instance, it seemed he couldn't advance any higher in his profession, because the head of the hospital was desperately afraid that he was of the Brotherhood. His wife died in childbirth, and he brought up his only daughter alone. Still, he always kept a positive outlook. He knew every beggar by name, and never accepted money from the poor. Yes, there are people like this. They are rare, but they exist."

"And?"

"When the military began to use live rounds, he thought he would uphold his doctors' oath. At the hospital they were arresting the injured demonstrators."

"I heard about that."

"It happened. The Mukhabarat pulled demonstrators straight from the operating table."

"What does this have to do with him giving up God?"

"When it dawned on Salem that the demonstrators would rather die on the street than come to the hospital, he and a few other doctors and nurses set up a triage in the Abu Bakr worship room."

"That's the one on the corner. I was there to take pictures. They operated on the prayer rugs."

"They slept on them as well."

Biled stood, closed the café door, then began to put the chairs up on the table. The sound of the chairs smacking against the plastic tablecloths roused the bugs that congregated around the table legs.

"They saw six hundred people a day."

"How do you know?"

He turned toward me and raised his pant leg. His ankle was swollen and purple. A long black incision ran all the way up to his knee.

"It didn't break, but I couldn't stand on it. It looked uglier than it was, so they placed me next to the burned and broken. The doctors were at it twenty-one hours a day then. Salem worked his fingers to the bone, stopping only to pray. The corpses were piled in the corner next to where they prayed, yet still they prayed."

"He must have been one of the truly religious ones."

"Indeed, but the patients were terrified of him."

"Because he prayed next to the corpses?"

"No, for another reason. As a surgeon, he only took the most serious cases. There was no medicine, no instruments. It was like out of the Middle Ages, the way they had to work. Sixty or so people died in his hands. It appeared to them that every person who he worked on died."

"And that's why he drinks?"

"That and more. The wounded cried for him to keep away. Some suffered from hallucinations, and they begged God not to let the Angel of Death touch them. I think it hurt him, because things like this can hurt a man. But it wasn't because of this that he abandoned God."

"Then why?"

"On the revolution's fourth day, the police shot into the crowd in Talaat Harb. The demonstrators brought in their wounded on blankets. By then, the work was routine for Salem. He laid the patients in an orderly line and worked on only those he thought he could save. But on that day, one of them, it turns out, was his own daughter."

"She was demonstrating on Tahrir?"

"Of course not. She was on her way home when she was hit by a stray bullet. She got it in the lung, and was already fading when they brought her in. Her father plugged the wound with his finger to stop the blood loss, and began to operate. All the while, everybody heard him speaking to God, how he said, 'Just this one, don't take this one. I was pure, I kept every rule; I never asked for anything. Just do this, I beg of you.' "

"And what happened?" I stood up to bring two more beers from the fridge. Biled lit another cigarette, sat down, and leaned back in his chair.

"He couldn't save his daughter. It was all over in half an hour."

"And that's why he drinks. He fell out with God."

I put the bottles on the table, and marked them on my bill.

"Or he discovered that no God exists," said Biled. He blew out some smoke and opened our beers. Ten more bottles would join our stream of drink that night.

The Devil Is a Black Dog

The moon rose high above the town, illuminating the clouds, the apartment buildings, and the hills beyond in a red glow. The air was cool, like it was every evening in the hills. There was no electricity in the town, just the blood-colored moonlight that gathered at end of the alleyways.

"It's like this from the storm," said Abdelkarim, when he noticed my expression of awe. "There was a storm in the desert, and the moon looks red from the dust."

He took a long drag from his cigarette. We had been coming out onto the roof most evenings since I'd moved into the mosque. It was good to sit in the night air, smoke hash, and talk about this and that. The government army had ended its shelling a few days ago. It was quiet now. Just the moon shone on the town, lighting up the destruction.

"Tomorrow the weather will be good," said the imam.

"How do you know?"

"My wife heard it on the radio."

I smiled and reached for the cigarette. Abdelkarim was in his early forties, but his beard was already gray. I had been staying with him for two weeks, since the day the Hotel Mecca was hit. The government had shelled the town indiscriminately, blowing the hotel to bits. When I'd come down from the hills, where I'd been staying with the Houthis, I found the building in ruins. The wretched hotelier, whom I managed to track down nonetheless, informed me that he couldn't return my two hundred dollars, because he needed it to feed his family. With no better idea, I knocked at the mosque where Abdelkarim was the imam. A big-hearted, generous man, he offered me a room. We immediately took to each other.

"What do you think? When will the foreigners return?" he asked.

"I don't know. Another week, maybe."

In truth, I had no idea.

The mujahideen controlled the roads, and kidnappings were common. My safest route back to the capital would have been to go with the armed convoys of the humanitarian organizations, but the soldiers had already evacuated everybody. I'd stayed behind, alone.

"There were many dead," said Abdelkarim. It was also his job to organize provisions for the wounded. He wasn't a doctor, but he could take their pain away; the town was awash with soggy, raw opium, brought from Afghanistan by returning mujahideen. The opium relieved the pain and induced good dreams. The mortally wounded could sleep until their hearts gave out. This was a merciful death for those who had been torn to shreds by gunfire, burned beyond recognition, or had taken a bullet to the stomach.

The wind caught Abdelkarim's robe as he stood up and reached out for the banister.

"Tomorrow the weather will be good," he said.

"Let's hope so," I said.

"I should take the girls out to kick a ball around. War shouldn't be their only memory of their childhood."

"Yes, that will make them happy."

He had two girls, one three years old, the other five. I frequently ran into them around the house. Abdelkarim allowed me to listen in as he read to them from the Koran and then explained the meaning of the passages. It was the wife whom I wasn't allowed to meet. That my meals were prepared and my clothing washed was the only indication that she lived in the house. Abdelkarim begged my forgiveness that he could not introduce me to her. A woman was not allowed to be in a room with a man who was not her husband or relative. Because of this, it was the custom in Yemen for new mothers to nurse their male infants together. They would sit in a circle and pass the baby from one to the next, allowing it to feed from each of their bodies, so they could all claim him as a relative.

"Let's go to sleep, friend. Perhaps tomorrow we can get a hold of a Saudi television channel and watch the soccer match."

"*Inshallah.*"

"I'll fix the antenna."

I tipped back the remainder of the *karkadé* that we were drinking. Bitter and cold, it stung the roof of my mouth. I took the pitcher in my hand and carefully, so as not to slip on the adobe stairs, started down. Abdelkarim followed, holding a gas lamp. Our shadows fluttered against the wall in front of us.

We arrived at the room where I slept, the floor covered in prayer rugs and horse blankets. There was no window, so there was no breeze, like there was on the top floor. By dawn, though, the room would be cold enough to see my own breath.

"Good night, friend," said Abdelkarim. "I will wake you in the morning." He shook my hand, then turned and began toward the floor below, where he lived with his wife. It was at this time that we heard a clamor coming from outside. Somebody was pounding against the mosque's green iron gate. We both rushed to the building's entrance.

Abdelkarim threw open the iron bolt and opened the gate wide. On the street stood a ten-year-old boy, barefoot and dressed in grimy clothing. From his belt hung an old Luger. His upper lip was quivering. He tapped his foot nervously. His eyes twitched.

"Thank you for opening the gate," he said.

"What brings you here, Abdul Muhyi?" asked my host. "And where is your clan?"

"The devil has come to the hills," said the boy.

That was the first time I heard about the black dog.

Abdelkarim lit a gas lantern on the wall of the prayer room, the light revealing a green prayer carpet. Abdul Muhyi sat against the wall and gulped water from a goatskin sack. The liquid dribbled down his chin and gathered in dark stains on his robe. He drank deep and long as we waited for him to continue his story.

"I was putting the goats out to graze by the cave tomb as usual," said the boy once he was ready. "I heard movement coming from inside. I thought somebody from the town had come to dig up a body, so I went in. The cave was dark, and at first I couldn't see a thing. . . ." His voice became clenched and he began to shiver.

"And what did you see, Abdul Muhyi?" asked my host.

"Bismillah, the devil! The devil was in the tomb in the form of a dog. He was eating human flesh and drinking blood." As he told the story, the boy's face strained with fear, and he paused repeatedly to recite the *Shahada*.

"And why do you think it was the devil and not just some stray dog? You know they have been hunting in packs up in the hills since the war broke out."

"His eyes glowed red."

"That's just how they look in the dark. I wonder why you didn't try to chase it away."

"But I did. I took my gun from my pocket and shot at him. I emptied the entire magazine at that demon, but he didn't move a muscle."

"And then?"

"It turned its head toward me. Abdelkarim, I have never seen such a sinister face in my life. It was like he was laughing. Like he was laughing *at me*. I began to run, I ran as fast as I could."

"I still don't understand why you think he was the devil," said Abdelkarim.

"He followed me all the way to the town outskirts. He only turned back when I said a Shahada. The name of the Prophet stopped him."

Abdelkarim went silent and stroked his beard. Finally he said to the young goatherd, "You are exhausted, friend. It seems we are all tired. Tomorrow we will look for the solution to this thing. Sleep here in the mosque."

Abdul Muhyi, still visibly spooked, took the imam's suggestion. We all parted ways to sleep.

The next morning I found Abdelkarim downstairs in the mosque. Abdul Muhyi was nowhere in sight. I washed in the well, then went into the prayer room, where breakfast was waiting. Abdelkarim's wife had baked bread, which was steaming in a basket. We ate it along with yogurt and cucumbers. I asked him about Abdul Muhyi.

"I sent the boy home," said Abdelkarim, as he tore into the bread.

"The kid was scared to death."

"I convinced him that his mind was playing tricks on him. The last thing we need are rumors about the devil. We've trouble enough."

"How did you convince him?"

"I told him that it was obvious to me that he hadn't seen the devil."

"And that was enough?"

"No. I also gave him my rifle."

"Why?"

"Because divine help was also needed. I thought I'd give him the gun and bless the ammunition. Now no more trouble will come of it."

"You convinced him your rifle can stop the devil?"

"It can stop this one. Mausers are good guns."

Abdelkarim poured us tea.

"Are you going to try to write an article today?" he asked.

"No. My laptop ran out of power."

"I'll plug in the generator."

"Don't waste the energy. Even if I write an article, I can't send it. The network is down."

"In that case, would you like to come with me to see the tomb in the hills? I need to get to the bottom of this before gossip starts. With two of us, it will go quicker."

"Of course," I answered, and went to wash my face. The water from the well was cold and left dark green stains on my shirt.

We traveled on Abdelkarim's beat-up Triumph 21. The paint was worn on the body but the seats were comfortable, because the imam was careful to keep them well oiled. It was a good little motorcycle and more than fifty years old. As opposed to modern Chinese trash, this one could withstand the climate, the night's frost and day's heat. He kept it stored under rough horse-blankets in the courtyard; it was well maintained, and he beamed with obvious pride when it roared to life that morning.

Abdelkarim drove, his robe blowing into my face when it caught the wind. We glided along, past the red hills; the black openings of the small caves looking like the gaping mouths of corpses. Red dust carried by the wind stuck to our sweaty clothing, leaving rust-colored streaks.

For about half an hour we wound our way down the serpentine dirt road that led to the caves where the tomb was. Since the town graveyard had filled up, the Saada people began to bury their dead in the hills.

Abdelkarim slowed down and came to a halt. The opening of the cave Abdul Muhyi had spoken about was in a hill above the road. We got off the bike and began to climb.

"Do the dogs normally raid the dead?" I asked as we hiked up the incline.

"More and more often. There are a lot of stray dogs. They go after the town's trash as well. But at the beginning of the war, there was simply nothing to eat in the town, so they came out to the hills to hunt. It seems they have also begun to mate with the jackals."

"I didn't think that was possible."

"A jackal is a dog as well, though we can say the stray dogs are more dangerous."

"Why?"

"Because jackals are still afraid of men, but dogs are not."

"What did Abdul Muhyi mean when he said the dog was drinking blood?"

"I believe it is just as he said. There is no natural water source, but where there are wells, there are also people. Any dog that dares to get near the drinking water is certain to be shot by the shepherds."

"That's why they drink blood?"

"That's why."

"So they don't die from thirst?"

"Indeed. Blood is a kind of water."

The cave's entrance was almost seven feet high; we both fit through comfortably. As Abdelkarim went ahead, I saw his hand poised on his robe. Over one of our dinners together he told me that he had been a soldier, and I knew that unlike the knives of people in the capital, the knife on his belt wasn't for decoration. It wasn't an especially ornamented dagger; the hilt of a red copper blade protruded from its simple leather sheath. The imam turned and took a gas lantern from the cave's wall. He looked for matches in his pocket to light it with. The pungent smell of congealed blood filled the cave and mixed with that of the gas.

Sand grated under the soles of our shoes as we went. Deep in the cave, spaces had been dug into the walls. They'd lay the dead there, and let the hot, dry air take care of the rest. The only problem was the linen sewed around the bodies. Since the offensive broke out, no new material had arrived in the hills, so what was left they used sparingly.

"What exactly are we going to do here?" I asked.

"It's certain that pieces of the bodies have been strewn about. We are going to put them back in the their rightful places."

"Out of respect?"

"Yes. And I don't want people to start gossiping. In this area they are terribly superstitious. All we need is talk flying around about the devil."

The light from the gas lamp flickered against the wall as we traveled farther into the cave. Soon we could make out the contours of the chamber where the burial places had been dug. We found the first corpse on the ground before us, upended on its side. The linen, brown with dried blood, was torn half away. Abdelkarim got on his knees by the body and placed the lamp on the sand. I stepped closer. The man's throat had been ripped open, his innards were missing, and his face was chewed to pieces. It was an ugly sight, one I didn't want to look at for long.

At least there aren't any flies, I thought, kneeling down next to Abdelkarim. I've always had difficulty stomaching corpses that were swarming with vermin.

"It was really a big dog," said the imam, pointing to the prints in the dirt by the body. They were as big as an adult fist. The animal must have been two hundred pounds at least. "It fed here. It fed on the flesh, and the rest was just for play."

"What makes you think so?"

"There are lots of prints here. I bet if you look over the bodies, you'll see that it just tore up the linen. This is big trouble."

"Why?"

"Because it got a taste of human flesh. It needs to be shot, because now it knows God created man full of nutrients, something we forget from time to time."

"Will the shepherds shoot it?"

"Yes. That is how it will be," said Abdelkarim, who then, from a pocket in his robe, extracted a stapler. He wrapped the linen around the man again and stapled it together. The snapping sound echoed throughout the chamber.

"Later, if the convoys return, we can rebury them with more respect. The Shura will designate a place in the city for a new cemetery; this is something we have already discussed. Now come on and let's get hold of him."

The body was stiff and easily lifted into the chamber.

We found four more bodies lying on the ground, and we moved each one. While we were carrying the last one, I felt something under my foot. I looked down and saw a 9 mm shell casing. After we put the body in its place, I picked the object from the sand.

"You know, I'm thinking about how Abdul Muhyi said he couldn't take out the dog with a bullet," I said, showing Abdelkarim what I'd come across. We gathered all the spent casings we could find.

"An animal of this size can't be taken out with pistol ammo," he said decisively.

I suddenly had a bad feeling, knowing that we didn't have a single firearm between us.

Abdelkarim again stooped over and began to count; and then, with long strides, walked over to the cave wall.

"Poor Abdul Muhyi never was the best shot in town," he said and pointed out the chip marks left by the bullets in the stone. The goatherd couldn't even hit a dog. We shared a smile and got ready to head home.

The sun was setting when we arrived back in town, and dark fell soon thereafter. The bike turned onto the road that led to the mosque. In front of the iron gate stood a crowd. They parted so we could enter. The women wailed loudly, and the men stood in a circle around where the boy's mutilated body lay. The shepherd had died clutching the imam's rifle.

With fingers numb from the cold I slowly buttoned up my jellabiya. Beyond the window the light of the torches flickered. It was already cold enough to see my breath in the room. The hills cast shadows over the courtyard. Down there the men were talking, though their words were distorted beyond comprehension from the wind. My face burned from shaving. I gazed into the bowl of water on my bed for a moment, and then took off my leather jacket and shirt.

Abdelkarim insisted that I take part in the assembly of men in the mosque, and he'd loaned me his festive jellabiya for the occasion, the one he had purchased for his pilgrimage to Mecca. It was worth more than my camera and equipment combined.

"For my greatly esteemed guest," he'd said, when he laid the robe in my hands. I was slowly getting used to how on certain occasions I couldn't show up in my Western clothing. Abdelkarim's friendship had greatly improved the town's esteem of me; I got fewer suspicious looks, and even the mujahideen mumbled "Peace be upon you," if we happened to meet at the market.

I didn't want to be late. Abdelkarim had calmed the terror-stricken crowd, and invited them to an assembly so they could discuss the case of the wild animal that was hunting among the hills. The men were already gathering. I fastened my belt, adjusted the *jambia*, the traditional dagger, and began down the stairs. By the time I got to the courtyard, everybody had already gone into the mosque. Only the clatter of the rifles that were hung on wall hooks could be heard in the wind. Abdelkarim didn't allow fire-arms in the mosque. I quickened my pace and took off my shoes. Inside sat about seventy men, loudly arguing. Abdelkarim waved me over.

I sat next to my host and quietly observed as some men squabbled, while others took to examining the corpse. They all agreed that whatever animal had done this to the shepherd needed to be hunted down. The town butcher, a mustached, pot-bellied man named Badr al-Din, shouted loudly that they should start for the hills at once, because "every lost hour is a waste." Many approved of his plan, though others thought it was a trap. A heated argument arose, with urgent gesticulations followed by many threats: exactly how Arabs typically argue. Abdelkarim strained to keep the tenor calm.

The ruckus lasted until Khaldun, a fifty-year-old, one-eyed mujahid, stood up. He wore a gray jellabiya and a long black scarf around his neck. His beard fell the length of his chest and his one good eye shined white with light. The old man had fought in the battle for Marjah, on the Afghani Taliban side. There he had lost his eye in a rocket attack; at least that's what he told Abdelkarim. They were old adversaries, because he believed my host was too lenient in questions of faith. He didn't go to Friday prayers in the mosque, preferring to pray at home, with the followers he came across in the town. He only attended the assemblies.

The old mujahid waited quietly for a few moments, casting his gaze over the others until they fell silent.

"Is it not possible that because of our guilt God has punished us?" he asked those gathered, his voice rising.

A shadow of worry passed over Abdelkarim's face. The room had gone totally quiet.

"We need to think about why he is punishing us with such a grave blow," the old man put forth.

"My respected Khaldun," said Abdelkarim, his voice stiffer than usual, "I note your concern, but the signs are unequivocal. A wild animal is hunting in the hills. Because it is night, and its tracks will be hard to follow, I suggest we set a trap tomorrow."

Many of the men voiced their approval.

Khaldun's face tightened, but he sat back down without another word. Badr al-Din offered to hunt down the beast himself, along with his boy. The produce seller, Safiy-Allah, also volunteered.

Finally, they decided that at dawn, after the Fajr prayer, the small party would leave for the hills.

I turned toward Abdelkarim and asked if I could go with the hunters. I wanted to see the hills again, and the desolate countryside. My host nodded, and said loudly, "Our foreign brother is volunteering to help with the wild animal's killing."

His announcement wasn't greeted with undivided enthusiasm. I saw old Khaldun shake his head disapprovingly, and look at me with spite. He hated everything and everybody from the West. To him, I was vice on two feet.

Badr al-Din decided the question. "Every bit of help is useful, from wherever it arrives. We agree to wait for our foreign brother in front of the mosque tomorrow morning," he said and, moreover, he appeared convinced that they really did need my help. The assembly, as always, ended with communal prayer.

I couldn't sleep from excitement, and by daybreak I was in the prayer room, ready to go. Abdelkarim and I repeated the Fajr prayer, and then went out to the front of the mosque. The street was empty. We stood shivering wordlessly next to each other, until finally Badr al-Din and his group appeared on the main road. They wore rough baize jackets and scarves tied around their heads. Safiy-Allah led a mule loaded up with gear. They greeted us with a "Peace be upon you." Abdelkarim handed me a shoulder bag. His wife had packed me some salted goat meat, onion, and bread. Off we went.

It was cold, and we had already reached the hills by the time the sun appeared. We didn't speak much along the way. Badr al-Din asked if I wanted a gun. When I said yes, he handed me an old World War 1 rifle. I thanked him and rested its rust-covered barrel on my shoulder.

After a three-hour walk we arrived at where Abdul Muhyi's body had been found. Animals were grazing there on the grasses that grew between the cliffs. The boy's blood had already dried in the sun; only the carcass of a goat with its throat torn out marked where the shepherd had been attacked.

Badr al-Din examined the tracks for some time. They ran north and turned off the dirt path. We followed them under the fiery, mercilessly hot sun. Sweat flowed into my eyes, and my shirt stuck to my skin. Safiy-Allah's teenage son gave me his scarf to tie around my head.

Badr al-Din lost the dog's tracks on a plateau. It was decided that we would ambush the animal there. It was a good place, because we could hide behind the rocks that abutted the hill, and the wind would carry the smell of blood in the direction the dog had headed. Each man grabbed a weapon from Badr al-Din as he unpacked the mule: modern Egyptian AK-47s, their barrels shining with oil. After we got situated, Safiy-Allah led the mule to about a hundred feet in the distance and tied it to a brittle, dead tree. He took his knife out and cut lengthwise into the animal's flank. The wound wasn't deep, but enough blood flowed for predators to smell. For two hours we lay on our stomachs between the rocks, waiting for something to happen, but the blood just drew flies, which flew in and out of the mule's open wound. The two teenage boys next to me began to chatter. Safiy-Allah and Badr al-Din ate the food they had brought. Time moved forward slowly. The moon appeared, and again we could see our breath as the rocks crackled with cold. Badr al-Din said that we would wait half an hour longer. The two teenage boys were already asleep in between the jutting rocks. I leaned against a boulder and gazed up at the moon. It appeared bigger than I had ever seen it. I could clearly make out the craters. Everything looked good bathed in its light.

First we heard a howling, then another in response. Soon, the night was filled with jackals calling to one another. The mule nervously clomped its hooves and pulled at its tie. I caught sight of five jackals approaching, their heads dropped cunningly, stalking the smell of fresh blood.

The men clutched their guns and waited. The animals were still too far away to get off a good shot. But before the jackals could attack, a large-bodied dog appeared on the hillside. Its huge silhouette stood out against the moon, and we could see the gleam of its tusklike fangs. When it began to bark, its breath came out in puffs that looked like smoke. At the sound, the jackals began to beat their tails. We watched, stunned. Badr al-Din was the first to regain composure.

"God is great!" he shouted, then began to fire. The others followed.

A barrage of gunfire scorched the incline. The cliffs showered stones—the mule was hit—but the black dog stood unmoving. He waited until the men emptied their cartridges, then skulked back into the darkness from which it had come.

"God is great! God is great!" the men cried in terrified voices.

Stumbling on the rocks, we started back to town, leaving the mule's corpse behind. Nobody had an explanation for what had happened.

Abdelkarim was still awake when I got back; he had been waiting for me. I explained to him what happened, then fell into bed fully clothed.

The next morning I found him in the prayer room, absorbed in the Hadith. The book he held in his hands was probably two hundred years old. Abdelkarim was wearing the same jellabiya I had seen him in yesterday.

"Last night the beast attacked and killed a woman named Khulud, and two of her children are in the hospital," he said. "One remaining child has yet to be found."

"Was it the black dog?"

"That is what they are saying."

"Now what?"

"I have to convince them once and for all that the dog must be killed."

The imam stayed buried in his book all day and didn't even emerge from the prayer room for lunch. I didn't want to bother him. Nor did I want to bring up the assembly that was planned for that evening.

The men, superstitious and fearful, listened to Badr al-Din's account of the hunt. The butcher, shaking a fist in the air, closed his speech by stating: "I am saying for certain that this dog is not of God. Safiy-Allah, his boy, and even the foreigner were witnesses." Terrified shouts of "God is great!" filled the room. Abdelkarim sat palely next to me, stroking his beard. He stood, and then addressed the men.

"My brothers. Listen to me, my brothers," he said. "We need to put an end to this dog before it kills again."

A numb silence descended. I could hear the oil lamp sputter and the clatter of the rifles against the wall of the room.

Khaldun stood up. "It's not certain that the dog is not of God," he said, looking over the attendees and then staring spitefully at Abdelkarim. "On the contrary. I think God sent this animal to call attention to the fact that we have strayed from the proper path. Those it killed, they were all guilty. Have you forgotten how many times you saw the boy intoxicated on khat leaves? How the husbandless Khulud was attacked, and her children as well?"

Men around the room began to nod.

"We have to put the question to ourselves: Why is God punishing us? The answer is here in front of us. It is because we have become lazy in our faith. Because God's commandments aren't fulfilled without err. Because we gamble, we don't supervise our women's morals, and we let foreigners into our homes. It is time to renew our submission to God, and examine the town's morality. Only in this way can we fend off these blows."

Shouts of "God is great!" broke out among the attendees. Many of those gathered stole a glance at me. Others hugged Khaldun and thanked him for showing them the light.

Abdelkarim sat wordlessly next to me, and when the tone had calmed, he stood.

"Excuse me, Khaldun, are you suggesting we improve our morals in the way they do in Marjah? Beating our women with sticks if their faith slackens? Stoning the criminals?"

"If this is the price of deflecting these blows from our heads, then yes," shouted the old man from his place. The surrounding men nodded.

"And if I guess correctly," Abdelkarim said, "you would nominate yourself to head a council of morality? It is known that you have had some practice in these matters."

"I only hope the brothers are humble and pious enough to carry out the task," said Khaldun.

"Yes, yes!" shouted the room.

Abdelkarim cleared his throat and continued. "Well, I believe you are mistaken, my respected Khaldun. We must kill the dog no matter what."

"Why need it be like this? Why is this how you want it?"

Abdelkarim stepped up to the butcher, Badr al-Din. "What color was the dog?" he asked. "Tell us, brother, what color was the dog?"

"Black," answered Badr al-Din, confused. "Black as night."

Abdelkarim leaned over and took the Hadith in his hand, the one he had been reading all day. He opened it and turned to Khaldun.

"We need to kill the dog, because the Prophet, peace be upon him, commanded it so. It says so in the Hadith: 'Kill the black dog, because the black dog is the devil.'"

He spoke calmly, and didn't raise his voice for even a moment. Again, quiet fell on the room.

"Respected Khaldun, are you suggesting that we shouldn't follow the Hadith?"

"I am not saying anything like that," the old man grumbled between clenched teeth.

He rose and left the room. Many followed. We could hear a religious song rise from the courtyard, their voices echoing through the alleyways.

"Who volunteers to do away with the dog once and for all?" asked Abdelkarim when quiet returned.

"Tomorrow morning we will begin for the hills again," said Badr al-Din. You could see fear on his face, but that he was gathering his strength. He liked Abdelkarim and had faith in him. Next to him, Safiy-Allah nodded.

"No, brothers," said Abdelkarim. "The beast is already hunting here in the town. We need to kill it here."

The plan was easy: the volunteers would hide by the hospital, where the smell of blood would be strongest. The men agreed.

The street was empty when we set off. The sky was dark; not a bit of light seeped in. Badr al-Din and Safiy-Allah went in front, clutching firearms in their hands. Abdelkarim and I took up the rear. I looked over my host's face in the darkness, but it gave away nothing about what he was thinking. I took out two cigarettes, lit them, and offered him one, but he didn't take it.

"Pray, brother, that we can kill the dog," he whispered as he pulled back the bolt of his Mauser, "or else Khaldun will have his way with this town." The rattle of rifle bolts locking in rounds echoed along the street.

We didn't speak again until we arrived at the hospital. It was a whitewashed, two-story structure. In the air hung the effluvium of disinfectant mingled with that of blood. The Dutch doctors had left when the government began a heavy shelling offensive, and since then the barber had been seeing to the wounded. The sun-beaten Red Cross insignia was the only reminder that foreigners once lived here. We could see the bodies of the moribund and unmovable on the blood-stained plank beds, asleep and breathing heavily under the influence of raw opium.

The hospital entrance was covered by a gray sheet. Badr al-Din was the first to enter. Because of the strong smell he tied his scarf around his face. After the first shelling, the locals had evacuated anybody who could move, so the hospital was almost empty.

Badr al-Din and Safiy-Allah positioned themselves by the sickbeds on the first floor. Abdelkarim and I went to the rooftop, where we had a good view of the area. We took our positions and waited.

"It is possible it won't come," I whispered to Abdelkarim after a tense hour. The moon was hidden behind black clouds and a strong wind blew across the hills.

"It must come," he answered, "in the name of God."

Another half hour had passed when we finally heard a screeching coming from a nearby street. The black dog, as though it had appeared from thin air, stood in the square by the entrance. Blood dripped from its mouth. At its feet lay the body of a girl.

Badr al-Din and Safiy-Allah came bursting out of the hospital, then opened fire on the animal. But the dog didn't flee; it just held its head toward the moon and began to howl, making a deep, thunderous sound that echoed through the streets. Twenty or so snarling mongrels appeared at the call. They stood behind the black dog and stared at Badr al-Din and Safiy-Allah with pitch-black eyes.

The black dog's muscles tensed and its teeth snapped as it sprang toward the two men. The pack followed.

"God! God!" yelled the men. They lowered their guns and stood paralyzed by fear.

But Abdelkarim hadn't lost his calm. He lifted his rifle to his shoulder, aimed, and let a bullet fly. It found the black dog.

The animal, which had until then seemed like it was swimming in the air, stopped short. It stood still and lifted its head. Badr al-Din and Safiy-Allah raised their guns again and began to fire. They dropped six of the mongrels, one after the other.

Transfixed, I stared at the black dog. It was gigantic. It shook its head and with a yowl charged Badr al-Din, blood streaming from its flank.

Abdelkarim's second shot also found its mark. The black dog stumbled. It tried to stay on its legs, but couldn't. The remaining mongrels from the pack fled when the black dog fell. It was still breathing when we arrived at the building's entrance.

Abdelkarim put a bullet in its head, and only after that did we examine the beast from up close. It was a mongrel, but unlike any I had seen before. It was probably over two hundred pounds. Countless old scars covered its muzzle, and flesh had overgrown both its ears. That's why it hadn't been afraid of the gunfire. It was deaf.

People filled the streets. Badr al-Din and Safiy-Allah threw the dogs' bodies in a cart, and the crowd accompanied them to the mosque. They left the bodies in front of the gate, so that in the morning the whole town could view the slain devil.

Badr al-Din invited everybody to celebrate the dog's killing, so we all went to his home. Abdelkarim, however, didn't stay with us. He begged our pardon, but he stated that he was exhausted and needed to return to the mosque.

I woke up to silence. I looked at my watch: it was four in the afternoon. The celebration had lasted until dawn, and I'd gotten home at sunrise.

I went down into the mosque, but couldn't find Abdelkarim anywhere. The house was totally empty. I went out into town, but the streets were deserted as well. It wasn't until I arrived at the hospital that I found where the crowd had gathered. There, where they had killed the dogs just yesterday, people were lying on stretchers, moaning, their torn clothing bunched up around their sweating bodies.

"What happened?" I asked a barefoot shepherd boy.

"It's a plague," he said. "Lots of people have high fever. They're throwing up and are breaking out in sores."

"Have you seen the imam?"

"He is inside with his two girls."

I cut through the crowd. The room was packed. The infirm lay on the floor or were propped against the wall, shivering with fever. I looked for Abdelkarim. I found him on the second floor. He sat on the tile next to a dirty mattress. On the bed lay his two girls, both unconscious. He didn't notice me. His eyes were glazed over and his face shook as he wept. I touched his shoulder. He looked up at me but it was as if he didn't know who I was. "We shouldn't have killed the dog" was all he could say.

I didn't know how to respond. I returned to the mosque. It was obvious that I needed to leave the town while I still could. In front of the mosque stood the cart, where we had laid out the dogs' corpses. I looked for the black dog, but couldn't find it anywhere.

The First

The soldiers arrived in a pickup. There were five of them; they jumped from the back and entered the grounds of the presidential palace, leaving the driver to wait. The building stood opposite a sickly looking tree, which gave cover to the men who sat on the sidewalk chewing betel and spitting. The men watched what was happening with interest. The smell of burnt garbage and fruit rotting in the sun wafted through the air: it was scorching hot, the start of the dry season.

The presidential palace looked like a Baroque castle, like a Versailles in miniature, with a park and fountains with swans in them. We could see it as we approached, descending from the hill. The machine gun nests and six-foot-high concrete wall were the only reminders that you were in N'Djamena.

The detainees were led into the courtyard. Three men and a woman, all black. Their hands weren't bound; they obediently followed one of the soldiers, who wore a red beret. He must have been the unit commander, because he was issuing orders.

The street had been blocked off by a military truck, and we wouldn't be able go around it without attracting their attention. Mustafa spat on the ground and turned off the engine, then leaned against the handlebars. "We'll wait," he said. "The restaurant isn't going anywhere." He was my fixer, a Muslim. He had arranged my stay in the city.

We'd wanted to spend my last day in Chad quietly. He had decided to treat me to some local cuisine. The restaurants were on the city's main street. We traveled on his motorcycle, as usual. Because of the truck, however, we would have to wait. From where I sat behind Mustafa, I watched the scene as it unfolded.

Without a word the three men stood by the wall; only their skin had become a bit paler and sweat beaded through their shirts. The woman began to shout. The man in the red cap kicked her legs out from under her. As she fell her shirt burst open, her breasts spilling out like two black water pouches. The other soldiers got a kick out of this and let loose with boisterous laughter. A smile broke out on the commander's lips, flashing snow-white teeth.

"What language are they speaking?" I asked Mustafa.

"Zaghawa, I think."

The conscripts slapped their knees as they laughed, pointing at the woman lying in the dirt. The woman began kissing the commander's black boots. The man enjoyed this for a bit, but when the woman wouldn't quit, he bent down and picked her up in his arms. The woman stood without protest. Her face was gleaming with tears. The commander said something to her.

"What's he saying?"

"I don't know."

The man extended his arm and pointed toward a car. With her head hung, the woman began toward it. She took a few uncertain steps, then stopped and looked back. The commander held his pose and mumbled something. The woman picked up her pace to the gate, pushed it open, and fled. The conscripts laughed loudly, and clicked their tongues to make their pleasure known. The man grinned widely. The other three prisoners stood silently by the wall.

The commander said a few words to the conscripts leaning against the truck. They took their rifles from their shoulders. These were Chinese-made Kalashnikov knock-offs, their wooden stocks oily from regular use. They cocked their weapons; we could well hear the click of the piston. They were taking their time. When they carried out these maneuvers they casually held their rifles under their arms. The commander fished his cigarettes from the pocket of his fatigues. He took one from the Fine Rouge pack, and then passed out cigarettes to the eager soldiers. The man lit up, then turned toward the prisoners. He said something and offered them cigarettes as well.

He stepped over to the detainees, smiled, and gave each one a smoke. They smiled and began to relax. The commander wiped his brow. As he walked back toward the conscripts he unsnapped the leather holster of his gun.

He held his pistol in front of him and examined it, perhaps to make sure it was loaded. Halfway toward the conscripts, he turned, extended his arm, and fired.

The sound of the shot echoed off the wall of the palace, and the birds burst from the trees. The commander had outstanding aim. The first prisoner was hit from ten yards, shot in the head, the bullet finding the forehead, passing through the skull, then caught by the wall behind. He died with a lit cigarette in his mouth. The other two men stared in shock. Then their instincts kicked in and they began to run.

They didn't reach the paved road alive. The commander sent a bullet into each of them. They were brought down by a shot in the back. On the ground their legs still kicked.

The commander reholstered his weapon, went to the truck, and got in. He noticed us and smiled, then signaled to the soldier next to him to drive. The motor kicked to life and in under a minute all we saw was the vehicle's disappearing outlines.

The remaining soldiers opened the gate and dragged the corpses away by their hands, heads bumping against the red dirt. In minutes the street was empty. The onlookers returned to chewing their betel, only that now the air was a bit sweet with the smell of fresh blood.

Mustafa kickstarted the motorcycle and we took off. We left the presidential palace behind, riding past tin huts and shops. It was already the dry season; the sky was an otherworldly blue. The wind caught our shirts as we rode, and I felt a little faint.

"We'll have fish, that's what I feel like eating," Mustafa said and turned from the main road toward Lake Chad. The air smelled of mud.

We came to a stop in front of a white adobe house, got off the bike, and went into the courtyard. White plastic seats and tables were set out on the beaten ground. There were no other customers. A Muslim woman in a flower-print scarf came to take our order. Mustafa chose for us fish with rice and a spicy tomato-pepper stew. He took out a cigarette, lit up, and offered me one. We smoked one each in silence.

"Are you still thinking about them?" asked Mustafa. "You look pale."

"Yeah. Who were they?"

"I don't know. They had the forehead scars of the Sara tribe."

"And that's why they killed them?"

"Perhaps."

"Why did they let the woman go?"

"I don't know."

"For fun?"

"Perhaps."

"They must have had a reason to kill them."

"We'll never know. It's useless to think about. Look at it this way: though they're dead, we are about to eat very well."

"Uh-huh."

"Especially because you are off to the frontier soon."

We went quiet. The woman came out and set plastic plates of food in front of us. Mustafa rolled up his sleeves, tore off a piece of bread, and used it to pinch up a piece of fish, which he dipped in the spicy stew.

"Aren't you eating?"

"I lost my appetite."

"Because of the execution?"

"Yes."

"You'll get used to this. And you will forget this. Now eat."

I ate. Then I left for Darfur, and from there went back to Europe, then to the Gaza Strip, Yemen, Libya, Nigeria, and beyond. It took six years. He was right, I got used to it, though I never forgot that execution. You never forget your first.

Taking Trinidad

The roof terrace, sir?" asked the hotel doorman. He was in the regulation red uniform with gold-colored buttons and a little black hat.

"Yes," I said. My smartphone buzzed in my pocket. I involuntarily checked to see what it was. Some girl commenting on Facebook; nothing interesting. But the device was useful in that it allowed me to cut short any further small talk with the receptionist. I didn't want him to ask how I was, what I did for a living, or why I was in the country. I didn't want to see him smile insincerely as he asked what I needed, then linger until I forked up a few coins as *baksheesh*.

A couple was also waiting for the elevator. I knew they were tourists, because they were in shorts, and only tourists wear shorts in Cairo. That's because everything gets coated by the dust and dirt kicked up from the street. And due to the unfathomable standards of Arab formality, nobody takes a person in shorts seriously, even in the city center. I've never liked tourists.

The elevator arrived quietly. Its door opened and we got in. My jacket felt tight around my arms; my muscles were sore after a two-hour workout at Gold's Gym. I looked in the elevator mirror and was pleased with what I saw. I was muscular but not overly buff. I was pressing two hundred pounds these days.

The doorman pushed the button for the fourteenth floor and the doors closed. As the piano version of "My Heart Will Go On" trickled quietly from the speakers, I reflected on whose decision it was to choose the music that plays in five-star hotel elevators. Why Vivaldi in the Four Seasons, Clayderman in the Hilton, but Celine Dion in the Marriot? Whose job was it to select the music that distracts a person's attention from the fact that they are racing up and down in a metal coffin at high speeds?

The doors opened at my floor. The terrace was bathed in afternoon light and the sound of gurgling water traveled down the leather-chair-lined corridor that led to the pool. The light wind blowing over the Nile brought with it the smell of mud.

Blue-and-white-striped patio umbrellas fluttered in the breeze. Just a few people sat at the bamboo tables beneath them, mostly Saudis. I cut across the pool area and headed for the bar. There stood a waiter named Omar, his shirt unbuttoned to his chest. He smiled broadly when he saw me. Omar and I were tight. I had been paying my respects at the bar for almost half a year now.

Omar was once an activist with the April 6th Movement. During the revolution he would talk about true democracy and the democratic transition.

After the army outlawed the April 6th Movement, he stopped talking about politics and took to drink. I knew this because his skin had begun to yellow, like that of all Arab drinkers. Their systems simply can't process alcohol properly.

"Whisky or daiquiri?"

"Daiquiri."

Omar nodded and took a bottle of Havana rum from the shelf. He poured a jigger into the blender, added ice cubes, and ground three limes onto a metal juicer that skillfully extracted the seeds. He shook the drink, poured it into a goblet, and then added sugarcane syrup.

"How was Sinai?" he asked, setting the glass in front of me.

"Good."

"It wasn't too hot?"

"It was. In Rafah it was up around 115 degrees."

"Did you see any tanks?"

"Yes. A few. There was fighting in El Arish."

"What kind?"

"The Bedouins kept the police building under fire for around eight hours."

"Damned Bedouins. I can't stand them."

"So the army came to restore order."

"Indeed, if the army showed up, order will follow."

My smartphone buzzed.

"Sorry," I said. Omar nodded and went to do some washing up.

The bank had sent a text. Two thousand dollars had arrived in my account; a pay transfer from the newspaper I worked for. I disconnected from both the mobile network and the Internet. I didn't want to hear from anybody. I looked at the cocktail in front of me, the condensation clinging to its side, and reflected that this had been my twelfth mission. I'd gotten it done, just like always. Not everybody could say the same. The fleeting image of Harvey Dabbs came to mind. In the Tibesti Hotel, in Benghazi, he was holding forth on the importance of prayer. We were drinking Johnny Walker, which they sold under the bar. The whole place was sloshed on it.

"You know, this is my fifteenth war," said Dabbs. "I'm in with God. I even have my own prayer. In this profession, you have to pray. 'Our father who art in heaven / hallowed be thy name / thy kingdom come/ thy will be done/ In war we earn our daily bread/ just don't shoot us with your "50s" / vests or not those buggers leave us dead.'"

"Amen," said everybody and applauded loudly.

A few days later, the Gadhafi loyalists began to shell Misrata, and Harvey Dabbs was killed. It was a stupid death, like every death in war. A car bomb had exploded next to him while he was photographing the rebels' advance. Three of us went to identify his corpse in the garage they were using as a morgue. Only his upper torso remained; the rest was lost to the explosion or stray dogs.

I pondered whether I should raise my glass to God's sense of humor or another stupid death. "To a stupid death," I said, and drank. I'd drink to a pointless idiotic death because, unlike God, it's something I have seen with my own eyes. The daiquiri went down well. I like to drink. It's good to drink after a war, during a war, before a war. It is good to drink with friends, to the death of friends, to childbirth, children's deaths, engagements and broken engagements, betrayal, quitting smoking, love. It's always good to drink. I signaled Omar to make me another. I looked up, gazed at the patio umbrellas rippling in the wind, the sand-colored Cairo rooftops, and laundry hung from the windows.

The second cocktail finally washed the taste of the desert from my mouth. I took out my smartphone and loaded the game *Sid Meier's Pirates!* I thought I should keep busy even if I had no real work. I had downloaded the game for free from the company's site; I got it as a bonus when I reached five gigabites of downloads the previous month, 200 dollars' worth.

I had begun to play the game the night before, to fill the six-hour trip from El Arish to Cairo. In the game you are a pirate captain. The goal is to retire with the most points by battling other pirates and marrying into aristocracy.

We got caught in a sandstorm on our way back through the desert. When this happens you can't see anything of the road, because the air is full of dark whirling sand. Nobody was in the mood to talk, so I just played. I began the game as an English buccaneer. It was going well for a few hours, but I kept getting stuck when I tried to take Trinidad. Four frigates from my flotilla with four hundred trained pirates waited in vain to attack, unable to overcome the tricky winds the game threw at us. I tried everything I could with the touchscreen, but my ships could only bob futilely in the sea as the city's red fortress showered them with fire.

I had to take Trinidad at all costs if I wanted to end the game with maximum points. In Trinidad there was money, Spanish silver, the governor's daughter. Everything you need to win. It bothered me that I couldn't find a solution, because I wanted to make the game's Hall of Champions.

I hate when I can't finish what I start. It saddens me to think I let an opportunity pass me by.

The menu came up on the screen and I killed the sound. I loaded my saved settings and began to direct the fleet, but again the wind worked against me. My entire fleet was sunk twice. I wondered if the problem was the weight, as there must be some reason the game notes just how much freight the boats carry.

Instead of frigates I need some lighter boats, I thought. *Lighter boats, which maneuver quickly, even in bad wind.*

"I think somebody's looking for you," said Omar, taking my empty glass. I turned. By the pool stood Alistair Bleakly, the *Independent*'s newly hired correspondent. He didn't look good. He was wearing the same clothing he had on yesterday in the desert. He hadn't shaved and his leather jacket sparkled with sand. I waved him over.

"I tried to ring you several times," he said, and hopped up on a barstool next to me.

"I was unplugged."

"You're a reporter. You should have your phone on."

"It's my day off. Why, did something happen?"

"I was just thinking things over. We should do something."

"About what?"

Alistair stared at me in dismay, but kept quiet because Omar arrived with the two whiskeys I had ordered. I looked into the boy's bloodshot eyes. He couldn't have slept much last night. We picked up our drinks.

"We should do something in regards to the woman."

"What were you thinking of?" I asked, and took a drink of the whiskey. "What should we do?"

"Well, we could notify the UN. About the things that are happening in Rafah."

"I'm not sure that's a good idea. You'd have to fill out a questionnaire of at least ten pages, and you would have to supply all your information. The whole matter would get to Amn ad-Dawla."

"I don't care."

"They deported people for less just last week."

"Then we might say something to the police."

"There are no police."

"Then the military."

"The military won't care."

"For the love of god, something should be done," hissed the guy through clenched teeth.

"You could put a paragraph about it in your report."

"That's all? They killed a person."

"It wasn't a murder; she was executed."

"Murder is murder. We should do something. We're reporters."

"You need to rest. You're exhausted."

"I can't sleep."

"I can see that."

"How can you stay so fucking calm?"

"I drink, work out, and I don't give a shit."

Alistair fell silent for a moment, then took one of my Marlboros and lit up. He had only just started smoking, and he had to make an effort not to cough. I used the opportunity to order two more whiskeys. I liked how they served whiskey at the Marriot, giving you the ice in a separate glass. Alistair tossed his drink back in one gulp. It took immediate effect; he probably hadn't eaten anything all day.

"I can't leave it like this," he said, more relaxed now. "You think I should write something?"

"Yes."

"But I don't even know the woman's name."

"Just write that it was a woman."

"Would you write that?"

"Yes," I lied.

"OK, I am going now. I need to talk with my editor."

"Good."

He stood and with quick steps started for the exit. His cigarette continued to smolder in the ashtray. I watched it for a bit, then picked it up and continued to smoke. I ordered another daiquiri.

He'll be alright, I thought. *He'll drink a few more and fall asleep. Or find a girl.*

I closed my eyes.

In Rafah a huge crowd had gathered in front of the Muhammad Ali Mosque. After the imam's pronouncement of adultery, the men of the mosque had dug a nice little pit. In it a woman was buried up to her waist. Her hands were bound so tightly behind her that she couldn't move. Her torso and head were covered with a flour sack, on which "UNRWA"—United Nations Relief and Works Agency—was clearly printed. It was surprising that the woman didn't say anything or shake with sobbing. She kept obediently still in the pit. She only screamed when, from no more than ten yards, her husband threw a stone. It was a big stone. Large enough to break a bone, but not big enough that the fun came to a quick end. A red stain rose on the sack where it hit. After her husband, the judges each took a turn; then the relatives, and, finally, the men from the mosque. She withstood a surprising amount. After the first few blows she was still lucidly proclaiming her innocence, until a stone must have broke her jaw, because after that she just whimpered, then finally went quiet. The pit was tight, so she couldn't collapse forward. The sack didn't tear open; it just became drenched with blood. The soldiers standing at a nearby checkpoint watched the whole thing disinterestedly. It wasn't their business to interfere.

"Do something," I snarled at him, and massaged my temples. I had taken a sip of the daiquiri, but found it sour. Omar had put in too much lime juice. *Do something.*

I turned to look around, but the bar was already empty, even the Saudis had left. Water was gurgling in the pool; the sun flushed red on the horizon.

I took my smartphone in my hand and reloaded the saved settings on the game.

Light boats, I thought. *If I trade my frigates, I'll be able to take Trinidad for sure.*

Something About the Job

Marosh knew everything about war. In the Balkans he knew when it was safe to leave cover, on the day when some seventeen-year-old sniper was taking two shots at every yellow press vest in the city because his mother happened to have slapped him that morning. He knew how to emphasize the "r" sound, like a Muslim, in the phrase *Assalamu alaikum wa rahmatullah*, the "Peace be upon you" greeting, when, for fun, the jihadist in Palestine put a gun to his head. He knew what a preemptive strike was, and knew that in war everyone was considered a woman, created with holes by a god in a bad mood.

He knew everything about war, or as much as one can know without participating in armed combat. He had no illusions.

If a young photojournalist found him in a bar and the topic of war photography came up, he shouted in English or in his unrecognizable Eastern European language, "Robert Capa and so-called humanist photojournalism is just a stupid joke, probably as unfunny as the Gospel!"

"These days every corpse has a price tag," he told the rookies. "A man shot dead is worth fifty dollars, a kid's worth a hundred, dead women are somewhere between the two. The world won't be an iota better if we show its horrors; at best we will give the good people something to waggle their tongues at as they empty their glass of orange juice at breakfast."

He never brought anyone with him to the field; he worked alone. He belonged to the bygone era of old-school photographers who were contracted by international news agencies, before the editors realized that the locals are cheaper: you didn't have to transport them to the region and they would do anything for hard currency. Furthermore, if they were killed, you didn't have to pay for getting the corpse home.

He knew everything about war. He was tall, almost 6'2", with a muscular neck and strong hands. He was salaried at an international news agency, where his pictures were appreciated, or at least published. He felt his life was okay, except for one small problem.

This problem surfaced in London, on a Monday morning, when he'd gone to the agency's headquarters to get a new assignment. As he waited for his editor in one of the leather chairs in the corridor, he looked over the photography collection exhibited on the wall, the company's wall of fame. Since the fifties, every picture that had received an award was hung there. He looked at a photo he had taken. Exactly above it was printed the well-circulated motto: "NO PICTURE IS WORTH A LIFE."

"Bullshit," he mumbled to himself. Then, finally, his editor Steve called for him. Steve was in his late fifties and visibly British. He leaned back in his chair and offered Marosh some hard candies before launching into a monologue.

Marosh knew something was coming, but he hadn't expected this. He was told that the company wouldn't send him to war again, because he was too old. "We have to give the young go-getters a chance," the editor told him in a paternal tone. "You can, however, participate in their training."

First, due to the surprise, he couldn't say a thing. Then came the anger. When Steve said that he was just "burnt out" and hadn't sent an extraordinary piece to the office in years, he just got up and left, slamming the door behind him.

Later on, he admitted to himself that what really pissed him off was the fact that Steve was actually right. Marosh was sitting in a pub near the office, thinking about his work over the past few years. He realized that in fact he hadn't produced any breathtaking images in some time. Not since Iraq—since the beginning of the war—when it seemed like it hadn't even been him who had captured such images. He had a theory that the man himself has nothing to do with the really important things. Something or someone else executes the creation, gives it—in this case, the pictures—a soul. Someone else made the exposure, someone who at that time and place took control. He couldn't explain it otherwise. How could it be that even he couldn't spot mistakes in his best images? He came to the conclusion that perfection has no characteristics. It just happens, if you're lucky enough. It can't be learned.

For a while, he considered himself crazy for having this theory, until he met a huge, gangling novelist at an award ceremony somewhere over a border east of Vienna. The crowd was there to celebrate Eastern European intelligentsia. The writer—who, at 6'6", could hardly fit into his chair—appeared increasingly uncomfortable over the course of the ceremony. The two of them were sitting in the last row and happened upon each other by the emergency exit.

By the time the master of ceremonies, whose calling in life seemed to be the handing over of prizes, reached the point in his speech where he proclaimed, "A few really great artists emerged in spite of the terrors of the former regime," the writer and Marosh were drinking bourbon in the closest bar.

After the fourth round the writer was telling Marosh that he didn't feel like he deserved any of the accolades. Writing a novel took him just three days, he said, when "the madness struck." Over the course of this time he couldn't see or hear properly, couldn't recognize his friends, and even addressed his lover by her last name. And, when the spell ended, he hardly recognized his own handwriting: it was like reading somebody else's manuscript. But the text was far better than any notes he had consciously produced.

"This is a goldmine," commented Marosh. "All you have to do is recreate the proper conditions, and there you go, a masterpiece awaits." But the writer explained that this is not how it works. Overcome with emotion, he told Marosh that he had been writing professionally for twenty years now, but during this time he managed to "touch God—or whatever you, dear sir, *Mr. Photographer*, wish to call it"—only once.

"It's pretty hard to knock on that door, you know," the writer said with an expression that made him look like he was lifting a heavy weight. "Obviously you can fool some editors for a while with the act, but not the damnable, faceless reader. But you already know this, I guess."

They drank until the event organizer found them and with a confused look told the two drunk men that it was their turn to step to the podium. Before they left, the writer gave his book to Marosh. *It's all just knocking at the door*, read the dedication.

Marosh took a sip of his beer and was contemplating what it was that he knew in the past that he didn't seem to know now. There were no compositional or technical problems with his pictures; no, he knew the mechanics well. Some intangible, poetic thing was missing, something that could transcend the daily dosage of horror. He knew when he caught the thing, knew the feeling. He just didn't know how to achieve it.

After his sixth beer in that London pub, when his ego was washed away by the waves of alcohol, he decided he would call Steve and apologize. He was suddenly overcome by a fear that others would also realize how burnt out he was, that other editors would put him out to pasture and he would never again be able to return to the theaters of war.

It was only there, indeed, in the middle of a war, that Marosh really felt free. The world simplified to "yes" and "no," to life and death. He liked how it clarified things, that there were no loans or credit, no competitors with better family backgrounds or better dispositions, that there were no chosen ones, and that everything was for the last time.

In his civilian life he felt like one of those whales that washed up on the shores of Brighton almost every year: he could breathe, but couldn't maneuver.

It took Steve a while to answer his phone, but he was an annoyingly good guy during the whole conversation. Marosh could imagine him standing in his patterned robe in the middle of his living room, scowling.

Marosh had no alternative but to agree to every condition. He would travel to Chad, a relatively calm African country, to escort a young photojournalist and familiarize her with the "rules of engagement" described in the company's guidelines.

Listening to his editor, Marosh swallowed one curse, then a second, as he felt a cold wave roll across his belly. His only response was, "What is the rookie's name?"

"Rachel Lynn," said Steve. "You'll have a hell of a time, 'cause she is quite a looker. It will be fun working with her."

Fuck me, thought Marosh, after he hung up the phone. He knew that type of female war correspondent. They were much crazier than men. They didn't heed god or man if it was about a story. They were able to put themselves at any risk, just to prove they were up to the job—and they were as good as any man. It was not uncommon for them to be shot dead or gang-raped by an entire company of soldiers if they were captured. He could clearly remember one woman in particular. Her name was Amanda, and she had been captured in Iraq. Marosh was sitting in the canteen when she returned from her release. It was 113 degrees in the shade, with flies all over the plastic tables. It was said that four men had raped her, but after her medical evaluation she was drinking Budweiser in the canteen, near to where Marosh sat, smiling. Marosh would never forget that smile. It was the smile of someone who knew that over the next couple of days all the news would be about her.

"Rachel Lynn," he grumbled, then asked for another beer and a whisky. He drank for a bit longer, and then took a taxi back to his hotel.

Rachel Lynn wasn't anybody's favorite, nor was she a Daddy's girl. In fact, she hardly knew her father, because when she was just five he died somewhere in the Middle East, having been beheaded by an extremist organization. In the eighties, a beheading was still a huge sensation in the media, and the press had been stationed in front of the family's apartment building for weeks. The family had to move en masse to avoid questions like "How does it feel?" "What are your thoughts?" and "Now, how will you carry on?" The front pages of the tabloids were meanwhile filled with the images of the execution, images cut from the video at the very moment they put the knife to his throat. That moment when a person realizes he is going to be killed.

Rachel's mother had her first nervous breakdown when the family lawyers told her she couldn't do anything to keep those images from being published. They were living in a darkened apartment and went everywhere in a car with tainted windows to throw off the reporters.

But, in the end, five-year-old Rachel discovered how her father died.

She had been playing on the playground of her kindergarten when a thirty-something blonde, cameraman in tow, sat next to her and asked: "How does it feel to know that your daddy was killed? That your daddy was killed in this nasty way by Mr. Terrorist? That he will never come back?"

Rachel wasn't thinking anything; she just kept her eyes on the blonde woman as she put the microphone to her face, and felt so alone that she couldn't move. Tears began to fall. The other kids watched the scene in silence until the blonde told the cameraman "Got it." They packed up knowing that the crying kid would look good as a closing sequence to the piece.

Rachel came down with a fever that night; her mother had to call a doctor for her. The channel eventually apologized, but only after airing the story.

A beheaded father and a mood-pill-dependent mother determined Rachel's childhood—though her father wasn't physically present, he filled the absence with his ghost. Her mother constructed a perfect myth from the man who remained unknown to Rachel. From the age of five she tried to please a ghost; this went on until she became a teenager, then she decided that she would become a photographer as well. Her mother almost threw her out of the house when she learned of Rachel's plan. Then, on a sunny Saturday morning, she told Rachel that she couldn't compete with her deceased father. That was the last time they talked to each other.

She wouldn't have it easy in her chosen profession, and all the friends of the family tried their best to turn her from her path. "One dead journalist is enough in a family," they'd say.

But Rachel was talented. Her pictures were nominated for prizes at every exhibition.

She studied at Oxford on a scholarship, but a contract with one of the photo agencies was far from assured. Her pictures just didn't interest the editors; her story ideas and notes lay unnoticed in folders on the desks of potential employers. Her failure lasted until she decided that in order to reach her professional goals she should use everything she had. Even her body.

The opportunity to apply herself arose with a low-ranking editor. She just let it happen.

Suddenly, all of her ideas were listened to as long as she endured the touch of the editor in some cheap motel room.

After the first occasion, she threw up in the toilet and showered for hours, but later on she learned to dispassionately use her body as tool. The midlife crises of men became her biggest ally. Rachel, at just twenty-four, became the most driven woman in every editorial office.

What she couldn't achieve as a freelancer at Burbanks, she achieved at Marosh's agency in four months. To lay the foundations of her career, she only needed to accept the dinner invitation of the chief editor and go with him to his weekend cottage in France while the editor's wife brought their kids to the grandparents. After just four months, she had a contract to travel to Chad to shoot refugee camps with a top photojournalist.

Marosh had flown back to Cairo. The summer was in full swing; the city felt like a gigantic blazing oven left open. He drank watery beers in a downtown bar, all the while thinking about how he could get back the thing that was missing in his photos. He spent a week walking the streets of Cairo in daytime, and at night he smoked hashish in his sweaty hotel room, but the solution wouldn't come. He checked his face in the mirror and found he looked older. His shirt was punched through with sweat in the warm summer night.

When the day arrived for his departure from the city, he packed his equipment, took a taxi to the airport, and caught his flight. He flew from Cairo to Libya and from Libya to N'Djamena. He took some snapshots for fun during the layover—but when he checked the pictures, he was so unsatisfied that he almost threw the camera to the floor.

He arrived in N'Djamena late at night. The city lay before him, unlit in the darkness of night. Marosh felt slugged in the head by the change in air pressure. He had tried several times to describe the difference between the sub-Saharan and Middle Eastern nights, but he never succeeded. In the heat of Africa a man does not sweat much. No, the heat seeps into your bones, your marrow, and changes the way you think.

The first day his feet had touched sub-Saharan soil he understood why genocide is so common in these countries. It's the air, its pressure—steamy and hot like fire, a heat that is experienced as cold by anyone who was there for the first time. It disturbs people's mindset, numbing it as the heat sinks into the cerebrum.

He caught a taxi at the airport and directed it to the Hotel Cosmos. He knew the city well, as he had been there during the civil war. The Cosmos was one of N'Djamena's best hotels, with its own power generator for nighttime. Chad was considered peaceful—the last civil war was ten years ago—and the rebel groups, which were divided by tribal background and were fighting the Zaghawa government, which was organized on a tribal basis as well, hadn't moved from the eastern part of the country in over a year.

Marosh had to wait a full day in the hotel for his female colleague to arrive, so they could begin photographing the country's camps, which were crammed with refugees from Darfur. He was suffering from terrible insomnia; the morning found him sitting in a plastic chair, terrified and shivering. Maybe he really had gotten old. If God didn't have something up his sleeve, well, this little trip to Chad might be his endgame.

Rachel disembarked from the plane, her skin almost sparkling from the strong sunshine. She wore jeans and a white blouse, the sweat immediately drawing dots onto her clothing. She teetered down the stairs from the plane and crossed the field with the other passengers to the airport. She filled out the necessary paperwork to get into the country, then traversed the terminal, which, with its dirty green walls, reminded her of a small-town train station in the English countryside.

She felt dizzy. Two weeks before her departure she had started taking Lariam against malaria. She debated the possible side effects for a long time, then finally decided to take it, ignoring the rumors about soldiers who went mad from the pills in Iraq; who upon returning home put bullets in their wives' heads, or, in the better-case scenario, their own.

She hastened through the terminal, avoiding the black-market money-changers' flashing eyes. Out in front of the airport she brushed off two taxi drivers, having to grab her luggage from out of their hands. Then she noticed Marosh.

The man shook her hand and offered to carry her bags, which she declined firmly. She bought a bottle of water in a nearby shop to ease her headache. The man asked if she would like to take a day to acclimatize, but this was out of the question. She wanted to fly to Abéché immediately, so they returned to the ticket counter to check in their equipment.

A small, two-engine plane was idling on the field, huge blue UN stickers adhered to its sides.

The two pilots were blonde, in their mid-thirties, and spoke with South African accents. Except for them and the two photographers, everyone else on the plane was black. Marosh took his seat first. Rachel sat next to him and fastened her seat belt.

"So you're the ones who are going to the refugee camps?" asked the copilot over his shoulder as the plane started to taxi.

"Yeah," said Marosh, nodding, his voice barely audible over the engines.

"Well, there is quite a bit of movement down there these days," replied the copilot, smiling. The plane took off.

"It's calm," said Marosh, looking at Rachel. "African calm."

Rachel looked back and tried to put a smile on her face, but couldn't. She could barely see from her headache, so she clenched her teeth. Each question he asked, like where she studied, had she been in Africa before, she answered tersely. She didn't initiate any conversation of her own for the duration of the flight. They flew two and a half hours east before the military airport of Abéché appeared. As they were landing they saw the French foreign legion's Mirage jets taking off.

A jeep was waiting for them at the airport. They got in and headed east to the UN base.

The reddish-yellow gravel of the dirt road crackled beneath the wheels of the car as they passed the white, low buildings in the streets. Small, scraggy trees stood in front of the houses; in their shade men in jellabiya robes were sitting and smoking. The air was filled with the smell of the nearby market, which the desert wind blew all over the city.

The UN base in Abéché was an adobe building, painted white with steel gates. Inside the fort walls there were well-tended flowerbeds and a canteen where everything was sold at European prices. The porter showed them their rooms. His face was decorated with horizontal cuts, indicating that he belonged to the Sara tribe. The two were given rooms opposite each other, both of which had a green mosquito net over the bed and a dirty fan hanging from the ceiling.

"Will he speak poorly of me?" wondered Rachel while unpacking her stuff and examining her camera. "No. He doesn't look like that kind of guy."

Seriously dizzy, she took a Lariam with two aspirin. She drank from a plastic bottle; the lukewarm water churned in her stomach.

The UN security officer held his regular briefing late that afternoon. Beads of sweat were glistening on his moustache as he informed those present about the current political situation. There were only a few people sitting in the canteen, mostly project managers and UN technical staff. Rachel had almost missed the briefing; she arrived drenched in sweat, and every movement took great effort.

"You've almost missed the show, girl," said Marosh, and indicated that she should sit in a plastic chair at his table. "Well, it seems our stay here will be quite interesting. The rebels are on the move, so the refugee camps are being evacuated. We'll get exclusive footage, because we are the only journalists here right now."

"Great," said Rachel. Red circles pulsed in front of her eyes, and she was having trouble catching her breath.

"That is, of course, if you don't get yourself killed. If you don't do anything stupid."

The man sounded like her family, her relatives. She envisioned her mother repeating those same words in her darkened room in London: that Rachel was just a girl and would get herself killed. Rachel's face clouded over.

"Don't talk to me like that," she said. She covered her mouth with her hand: she felt nauseous. "I'm here as a professional photographer," she continued, regaining her composure. "I took the safety training; I know exactly what the rules of engagement are. I know everything about the job, and fought my way to be here."

"And I'm here to supervise you."

"That doesn't give you the right to talk to me like they talk to interns at the agency."

After she said her mind, Rachel stood up from the table and walked out of the room.

It was getting dark, and the base took on a yellow pallor from the overhanging lamps. Insects attacked the light bulbs in swarms. The public faucets on the walls were full with them, and their buzzing could be heard all around the base. Marosh gazed after the woman for a while, then stood up and went to his room as well. While unpacking his equipment, he considered that, practically speaking, Rachel's outburst was justified; he had no right to treat her like an underling. He was the one responsible for the current situation. He was the one who no longer felt the craft in his hands. He felt awful for talking to the woman like that.

Rachel was lying under the mosquito net, sweat imprinting her contours on the sheet. The air conditioning hadn't worked in years, and the fan only stirred up the hot air. In her dream, she saw herself from the outside, at the age of five. She saw that little girl who was being asked how it felt not to have a father anymore. She saw herself alone, weeping. The loneliness of the dream lasted for a long time afterward.

Finally, another image emerged. She saw her father as he reached over her, caressing her hair and saying everything would be fine, because he had brought medicine. "It will just be a pinprick and everything will be alright," her father said. "You won't remember a thing by next week. This happens quite frequently at the equator."

She saw the man sitting at the end of her bed; she felt his hand holding hers. "I hope I didn't hurt you much. I didn't mean to be rude to you," said her father, who then wiped her forehead with a damp handkerchief. His voice was quite gentle.

"No hard feelings," said Rachel. She didn't dream anything else that night.

In the morning, Rachel got dressed, threw her backpack over her shoulder, and left her room.

Marosh was waiting for her in the canteen. It was eight o'clock and the sun was already beating down. Breakfast was served on aluminum plates. The humanitarian workers were having bacon, eggs, and assorted vegetables. Marosh couldn't eat anything; he just sipped a coffee and knocked the ashes of his cigarette into an empty Nescafé tin.

"When do we go?" she asked, taking a cigarette from Marosh's pack.

"Twenty minutes or so," answered the man, lighting another cigarette.

"Great. I think I had a fever yesterday."

"That happens quite often at the equator."

The whole staff at the base was preparing for the evacuation from Abéché, waiting for the order from the security officer. Foreigners were allowed to stay at their own risk; only a few had returned to N'Djamena—the sort who took UN protocol literally and would cover a five-yard distance between two buildings by car just to be on the safe side.

The rest had stayed.

Excited conversations struck up around the tables.

"I've got a driver who will go to Goz Beïda," said Marosh, standing up from the table to stretch. "But I think it would be better for you to stay at the base until you feel better."

"I'm fine," responded Rachel. This was, of course, not true. She was shivering and felt horribly weak. The dizziness returned as she rose from her chair, but Marosh didn't notice.

"OK then. Let's go."

They walked out of the canteen, crossed the parking lot, cut between a row of dusty jeeps, then exited through the base's steel gate.

Marosh felt a knot in his stomach when he remembered he would be taking pictures. He had to tell himself that he could get it back; all he needed was to get into the routine again. He didn't need anything else, just the goddamned routine—the rest would be done by the programming in the camera. Over thirty this was generally true about everything, he thought with a smile. He watched as Rachel took out her Canon 2D—the same machine he had worked with in Iraq. *Maybe the young can make it, after all. Maybe they're not so covered in shit that God can't see them*, he thought, as he took out his own Canon and took a photo of Rachel.

The driver was called Zeyad. He drove the car barefoot, chain-smoking Fine Bleu, the only brand sold in this country. He was going to Goz Beïda to bring back the humanitarian workers who had stayed in the field. There were three UN workers in the refugee camp, all of them locals; having received some humanitarian training, they were there to give the Sudanese women instruction in hygiene and general counseling.

Goz Beïda was thirty-seven miles from Abéché and accessible only by a dirt road. Not a single government soldier was to be seen in Abéché; they had already retreated from the advancing rebels. The jeep's wheels stirred up the dirt as they drove on a sandy plain dotted with dark green shrubs. Rocks emerged from the horizon in red, looking like ruins under the blue skies.

"This would be such a beautiful country if it wasn't for the war," said Rachel. None of the men responded; they just watched the landscape go by.

They drove for an hour on the dirt road, crossing over dried-out riverbeds. The caked mud crumbled under the jeep's wheels. They had to cross a shallow river before reaching Goz Beïda. The water splashed up between the wheels. It was a dying river, one that would dry out in days, the last remnant of the rainy season. Rachel opened her window and let her hand fall into the water, which felt lukewarm, like blood.

She didn't feel any better. The headaches and dizziness from yesterday had returned. She wanted to keep her condition hidden from Marosh. But the man wasn't paying her any attention; he was busy watching the donkeys as they drank, tethered, with bowed heads.

Marosh was thinking that there was no hope: *God cared only about the young.* If God existed at all, that is, he didn't give a damn about burnt-out photographers. He looked back at the woman and caught a look of almost unfathomable determination on her face.

Not long after they crossed the river, the refugee camp came into view. It was bigger than any city in Chad. The sandy spot where it was situated was covered with okra. The cornlike plant's green leaves clung to the huts and tents.

When they arrived, they saw that a huge crowd was gathered in the middle of the camp. Almost two thousand people crammed in together, entire families, waiting to be evacuated. The men and women were holding their few earthly possessions on their heads, all the while shouting and swearing, as the children wailed. The air was filled with the stench of human sweat and animal dung.

They got out of the car and agreed with the driver that they would meet by the riverbed no more than two hours later. They wanted to leave Goz Beïda before the crowd.

"Stay with me," Marosh called over his shoulder to Rachel, but she wasn't listening, and had already gone off in the other direction. Both started to take pictures.

Rachel skirted the crowd to where the huts and okra fields began. She felt her fever burning; her shirt was soaked through with sweat. She noticed a family of three. The father walked ahead, behind him trailed the mother, cradling a three-year-old child in her arms. The girl immediately stopped crying when she saw Rachel. Rachel smiled at the kid, and then took their picture.

No one knows who started the shooting. Maybe the local militia shot at an aggressive refugee, maybe rebel scouts had reached the camp. Chaos broke out when the machine-gun fire started to crackle. Flashes came from the okra field, the air filled with the sound of gunfire and the cries of the wounded. The point where the refugees had gathered emptied out in a minute; only the dead and the wounded remained. The camp's militia returned fire from the riverside.

At the first sound of gunfire Rachel started to run with the family in the direction of the okra fields. The man was running in the lead, and his chest was torn through by a salvo of fire, his falling body knocking Rachel to the ground and streaking her face red. The mother and child lay thirty feet ahead of her. The woman had taken a bullet to the head, her belongings scattered on the ground where she fell. Her child, eyes wide open, was sitting next to her, staring at her mother. She didn't cry. Rachel's view was obscured by flowing blood, but not her own. She felt light as she watched the child. She took a deep breath, pushed the body off, and sat up.

Marosh had taken cover about thirty yards away. His experience had helped him to dodge the line of fire: at the first sound of gunfire he had ducked and crawled to cover. In the early chaos, he couldn't see Rachel, so he took pictures of the fleeing, terrified people and the bullet-riddled bodies falling to the ground. When he felt he could guess the positions of the shooters, he started to search for his colleague.

At first he wasn't able to spot her, because she was hidden under a body. *Good God*, he thought, *if this woman dies, I will get crucified in the office.* He checked the area nervously, but couldn't see anything. *If she took the safety training, then she knows what to do,* he thought. Then she wouldn't run into the crossfire with the others. He leaned out from his cover to get a better look. *She is my responsibility. She's got no experience in the field. I'm responsible for her life. I must take care of her.*

He noticed Rachel when she sat up, not far from the okra field. She stood and began to run in the direction of a child. He knew he should shout, that he should yell something like "Stay down," or "Forget the kid!" or stand up himself to buy her time, to distract the attention of the soldiers. But he didn't do these things.

Marosh felt a familiar vibration and he was suddenly overcome by a deep tranquility. He raised his camera, zoomed in, and took a picture of the woman running toward the kid. He shot the whole sequence, as she crawled through the corpses and her shirt became stained with blood. He continued to shoot when she reached the child and gathered her into her arms.

Then the soldiers commenced their final assault.

How We Didn't Win

He had been given a place in the trauma unit in the hospital's new building. It was light there, warm and spacious, and smelled of disinfectant and paint. The old hospital with its flaking plaster walls and neon lighting wouldn't be missed. If we felt trepidation out front, it passed when the elevator door slid open. The old, creaky equipment was new and strong. Balint hummed a tune between his teeth as we ascended. It was almost two on a Friday afternoon. We were going to visit a friend of ours who had been laid out there for a week. His mother said he was coming around, and the doctors had taken him off sedatives. Despite the rib and skull fractures, his young system was bouncing back.

"The whole thing is his fault of course," said Balint, pushing his hands into the pockets of his bomber jacket and checking himself in the elevator mirror. He shifted his weight from one leg to the other, looking intently at his own reflection. The jacket was a really nice one. He had bought it at a hooligan store in Vienna, on Mariahilfer Strasse. He got his belt there, too, which flashed as he straightened his clothing. The leather was covered with metal studs, so you could wrap it around your fist if you needed to hit somebody. It was practical garb: the security couldn't confiscate it at soccer matches, and they knew it wasn't worth trying, if you see what I mean.

"Is that how you want to kick things off?" I asked.

"Of course not," said Balint. He looked away and began to air box. "It's just good and clear where this stupidity is leading."

"Try to be nice, okay?" I thought about what I would say.

"Okay," said Balint and unzipped his jacket. I thought of Chaba. It wasn't his fault he was this way. He was simply trying to fit in. I sometimes think Balint allowed him to hang with us out of pity: he was obviously the weakest in the group.

The door opened, letting us out on the corridor of the trauma unit. To our right was the reception area, with a computer, telephone, and white desk. Behind the counter sat a bleach-blonde girl around our age, reading the paper. When she heard the elevator bell, she looked up at us and smiled.

"Hello, we're here for Chaba Horvath," I said and smiled back.

"Uh-huh. The boy in room six. He's had a busy day. This morning the police were here for him as well."

"So he's in six?" I asked and looked at Balint. He didn't say anything, but it was obvious what he was thinking.

"Yes, at the end of the hall on the right."

"Just relax," I whispered to Balint. I hoped he wasn't going to make a scene. Chaba didn't need anybody to tell him how lame he was right now.

"I am relaxed," said Balint, and we started for the door.

Chaba had been very proud of his new viper baton. He'd pulled it out a number of times in the high school bathroom where we used to go to smoke, to show how fast he could strike with it. It even had a leather holder. He'd always been a nervous kid. He'd stood in the bathroom with a cigarette in his right hand, the viper in the left, and explained that if he hit anybody with it, it would definitely break a bone. He'd only had it for a week, but he carried everywhere. "Here's how I'd bash those dickfaces' heads in," he said, and struck the wall. Indeed, the tile shattered where it hit.

Balint didn't like the thing, and he let it be known. He'd told him: "Chaba, you're not the type to bash a guy's head in straight away. It would suck if somebody grabbed it from your hand. Better to give it here before somebody beats the shit out of you with it." Chaba didn't say a thing, but you could see he was hurt that Balint didn't trust in his skill. He took it with him every time we went partying, but he never had the chance to prove himself.

We arrived at door number six. Balint paused, then turned the knob. We found ourselves in a four-bed ward, with little tables next to the patients. The room was painted a genial eggshell color. Chaba's mother had put roses on her son's bedside table. She came every day to fold his light green blanket at his feet and put his brightly colored pajamas in the dresser.

Our friend's bed was by the door. An old man was in the bed by the window, wearing a cast that came up his thigh. He was asleep. The other two beds were empty. Chaba really *was* awake. His torso was totally encased in plaster. His head was swaddled with bandages. What was visible of his face was purple: his two black eyes were also bloodied. The doctors had fastened his left hand to the bed, and it had been screwed in multiple places so it would set correctly.

"Hey Chaba," said Balint in a chummy voice.

"Hey guys," came the raspy, faltering answer. His ribs were broken. Every word looked like it hurt.

"You don't look so shitty," began Balint, adding, "under the circumstances."

"Yeah," answered Chaba. "The doctors say I'll be alright."

We went quiet for a few moments and gazed down at the boy lying on the bed. We didn't know what to say.

"What did you tell the police?" asked Balint, breaking the silence as he leaned against the wall.

"Well, not that they fucked me up with my own viper."

"Then what?"

"That it was *unknown assailants* behind the Colosso."

"And?"

"Now they are looking for unknown assailants."

"You didn't mention us?"

"No, of course not." He wheezed when he exhaled.

"Okay then."

"Sorry we weren't there that day," I said, avoiding his gaze. Instead I had fixed my eyes on a point in the cast, talking to that.

"Yeah, me too," said Chaba. His voice betrayed no feeling.

"But you know who they were, right? Do you know who did this, Chabi?" asked Balint.

"Not by name. But the leader was a kid from the boonies, I think."

"What did he look like?"

"Big and bald."

"That's all?"

"That's all. Except he had a tattoo on his neck."

"Would you recognize him if you saw him again?"

"Yeah."

The conversation was obviously wearing Chaba out, because he began to gasp and sputter. We didn't want to push him. We gave him the porn mag we had brought as a gift. We said we would come again tomorrow, and before stepping out of the room we coaxed a smile out of him by adding that in the meantime he should hang in there, because without him we were one player short on the field. We walked wordlessly to the elevator at the other end of the hallway. We waited a little, and then got in.

"This isn't right," said Balint, when the doors closed.

"No, it's not," I said. "They got him good."

"He didn't have a snowball's chance." I saw a vein swell on Balint's neck.

"What now?" I asked.

"Now we get ourselves together, and tonight we go and take the fuckers out."

"Yeah, but you know, it's obvious Chaba fucked up. He whipped out his viper and fucked it all up."

"It doesn't matter."

"Why doesn't that matter?"

"What matters is that they fucked with one of us."

"And?"

"Now we are going to fuck with them right back."

"Why?"

"Because the whole is pointless without the parts."

"And if one part was stupid, does that still hold?"

"It holds."

We got off the elevator and strode from the hospital, then cut down the path between a row of willows. Patients were sitting on the benches, smoking or strolling with their visitors. It was one of the last warm days of autumn; the leaves had already fallen and were piled in the streets. Neither of us spoke.

I wavered a bit on what to wear, finally deciding on my steel-tipped boots. I knew the weight would inhibit quick movement, but I also knew a kick with them could break a bone. I looked over my mini baseball bat as well. It had the words "wood conditioner for dark skin" burnt into it. Something stupid I got from a friend with the pledge that we would fuck up some gypsies. We laughed: we didn't really know any gypsies. Finally I decided against bringing it because of the bouncers and police. It's never good if they find things like this on you during an ID check.

Balint came over at nine that night wearing the same clothes as earlier. His hair was gelled back and he had taken out his earring. "Ready?" he asked, and lit two cigarettes while standing on the threshold. "One second," I said, and told Dad, who was watching a war movie on TV, that I would be out late. Then I grabbed my leather jacket and left.

We went by foot to the Colosso. Along with the other clubs, it was at the opposite end of the city, out by the factories. We could see our breath in the air; it was a good twenty-minute walk. We didn't say anything as we went. We always quieted down when we were about to fight.

There was already a crowd in front of the Colosso: high-schoolers, factory workers, folks from the nearby housing developments. Drum and bass poured from the open doors out onto the street. A strong smell of weed came from the cars, kids getting primed for the night. The girls were in heavy make-up and skimpy outfits, chatting away with the guys. Behind the disco, the last packed train of the night departed, the ground rumbling under our feet.

A few acquaintances invited us to smoke, but we passed them by. We didn't stop for a single hit: we needed to keep our heads together. I already felt the music throbbing in my guts.

We paid the cover and hurried straight past the bouncer sitting at the door, cut across the crammed dance floor, and went over to the bar, where we ordered vodka Red Bulls.

"What do you think, will they be here?" I shouted to Balint.

"They'll be here," he said, leaning into to my ear. "They're always here."

"And when we see them?"

"We'll fuck them up."

"What's that supposed to prove?"

"It'll show that you can't fuck with us."

"Why is that so fucking important?"

"We don't have many friends. It's as though they fucked up you or me. You'd swing for me, right?"

"Yeah, but you wouldn't have done something so stupid."

"Of course not. But *if* I did something that stupid, you'd take them out, right? That's why we're friends."

"Yes, most likely."

"In friendship it doesn't matter if your friend is stupid or not. It only matters that you stand by each other. It's one of those things, like you never hit a woman."

We waited at the bar for a bit longer looking through the crowd. There was a lot of commotion; the dance floor was packed. I watched the girls shake provocatively as they danced, the guys sipping their drinks and hitting on them. Sometimes a pair would stop dancing to make out, the guy holding her by the ass.

I didn't notice when Balint took off; I just looked over to the side and realized he wasn't there anymore. I ordered another drink and began to look for him in the crowd.

I spotted him standing on the other side of the dance floor. He was staring at a group of three guys sitting in a booth. They were bald, wearing bomber jackets and boots, and talking to two girls they knew. The girls, in miniskirts and with bad dye jobs, giggled at their jokes. One of the guys, looking six feet and two hundred pounds, stood up and took a girl to dance. He removed his jacket, revealing a white singlet. The tattoo was clearly visible. It was an abstract design that began at his neck and ran down to his hand. Balint looked over to me and nodded. I nodded back. I turned toward the bar and ordered a bottle of wine. The bartender asked what kind and I said the cheapest. He gave me a bottle and I asked for two glasses. I filled both full, and drank the rest from the bottle. I didn't let Balint out of my sight for a moment.

Balint waited for the guy to begin to dance with the girl, then made his move. He used a well-worn trick—an old but good one. He began toward the pair, and when he was alongside them he bumped the guy with the full force of his shoulder. I watched the two begin to gesticulate, the girl standing between them. I saw Balint point toward the exit. The boy, red in the face, nodded vehemently. They started for the door. His friends sitting in the booth stood and went after them. I grabbed the bottle and followed. I knew we would win; I felt it in my gut. At times like these we always win, because we never ride free. They wouldn't even know what hit them. They weren't prepared: they hadn't shown up ready to be outnumbered, and they hadn't been careful not to drink too much. They had no idea that we'd been waiting for them all night. A person who can measure the balance of power knows what to look out for, what kind of resistance or attack he can expect. It's like riding a bicycle. It's only hard starting out. But once you are used to it, you can get into a fight already having been told everything you need by the posture and the movements of your foes, and even by what they are wearing. Chaba simply hadn't learned any of this.

But we had.

Because of the crowd it took me longer than I had counted on to find them. Outside, I cut across the parking lot and headed toward the embankment, where they were already getting into it. Balint and the guy stood shouting loudly at each other, grabbing each other's clothing in a tangle of limbs. The guy's two friends arrived as well. One began kicking Balint in the back, though it didn't seem to faze him. Next, the other jumped Balint from the side, taking him to the ground. They were just about to surround him, to stomp on him a bit, when I arrived with my wine bottle. I ran toward them so my blow would have the greatest impact, and with the sole of my boot I kicked one in the spine, sending him flying a few yards. Without waiting for them to react I swung at the tattooed guy's head with the bottle. It shattered against his left temple, leaving just the jagged neck in my hand. He staggered backward a few yards, and then collapsed.

The third guy turned toward me. He spotted me starting for him with the piece of broken glass in my hand. Before he could charge me, Balint got him from behind, grabbed his neck, and clamped his head forward. It was a commando hold, one we had practiced in the school bathroom. After a few good seconds, the brain can't get enough oxygen. There was terror in guy's expression when he realized he wouldn't be able to get free. He was on the ground in under ten seconds. Balint grinned at me. I saw his teeth were bloody. We heard the sound of the boy's boots on the cement as he fled the scene.

We set on the guy with the tattoo. I kicked him twice to wake him up. He tucked into a fetal position, shouting, "Don't hit me!" Balint also kicked him a few times, not sparing his head, because Balint wasn't wearing his steel-tips. The boy's face was a bloody mess. His nose was broken, and shards from the bottle left their mark on his cheek. Balint straddled his chest and began to beat him until he couldn't speak. The hot blood steamed in the air. Balint got off him, fists covered in red. The guy was still breathing; we saw the rise and fall of his chest.

"Break his hand," said Balint, panting. I jumped on the guy's arm with all my strength. I lost my balance from the force of the blow and staggered backward.

"Sure it's broken?" asked Balint, wiping the blood from his hand on the guy's singlet.

"I don't know. I didn't hear the crack. They usually crack."

"Take another shot."

I took aim and kicked. No sound.

"Wait, I'll lift his hand. Aim for the wrist, that will do it for sure." I stepped back a few yards to wind up. Balint lifted the guy's hand and held it in the air. I ran toward him and kicked. The steel tip hit exactly on his wrist and we heard the crack of the bone. Balint let the hand drop and it fell, twisted, on the ground.

"Do you have your cell phone on you?" he asked, still panting. He spat some blood on the body.

"Sure."

"Take a picture."

It was dark out, but the phone light was enough to illuminate his face.

We arrived at the hospital around three the next day. On the way it occurred to us that we should bring a gift, so we stopped at a gas station convenience store and bought some chocolate. Balint's hand was wrapped up, like always after a fight. He could hit correctly for the first few swings, but after that the madness took hold and he stopped paying attention.

We knew we couldn't go near the disco for a few weeks because the paramedics had to file assault charges due to the great bodily harm we'd inflicted, but this didn't bother us one bit. "We really gave them what they had coming to them," Balint said in the elevator and patted me on the back. "We needed to."

"They got what they had coming to them," I said with a grin.

"Hell yeah."

We arrived at the trauma ward. The same blonde as yesterday was at reception. She gestured that we could proceed. We strolled down the hall and opened the door. Chaba had company. His mother, a woman in her fifties with a red dye job, was standing over him. She was saying goodbye.

"Now here are your friends, darling," she said, sounding touched. "Chaba said you come regularly. You really are good friends, really." She said goodbye to her boy and left. She had afternoon work cleaning offices, on weekends too. There was no avoiding the two sloppy kisses she planted on our cheeks.

"Sorry for my mom. That's just how she is," said Chaba after her footsteps disappeared down the hallway. He was in better shape than yesterday. He could even sit up.

"No problem," I said. "That's just how mothers are."

"When do they say you can return to school?" asked Balint.

"Four or five weeks."

"That's a fucking long time."

"Yeah. I'll be home schooled like the other fuck-ups, I think."

"They got you good."

"Yeah, real good."

"Show him," said Balint. I reached into my pocket and took out my phone. I clicked on the picture, and held it in front of Chaba's face.

"Recognize this cocksucker?"

Chaba leaned toward the screen. He looked at the picture for a long while, and then shook his head.

"No. Never seen him before. Who is he?"

We stood looking at one another for a few moments.

"This is the cocksucker we messed up yesterday. Nothing more. Just some cocksucker," said Balint wanly.

"You guys are hard. Fucking hard," Chaba said and leaned back.

"Yeah," I muttered. We said goodbye because we could see Chaba was tired.

We both kept quiet on the trip home; there was nothing we could say. We just smoked and stared ahead. Balint lived in a housing development outside of town. My parents' flat was on the road that led there, so he walked me home.

"Okay, later," he said, then carried on.

At nine he returned in a beat-up Golf he had borrowed from his older brother.

"I was thinking we could cruise down to Csorna," he said, grinning as I opened the door.

"Why not?" I said. We got in the car.

On the way to Csorna—a small town an hour and a half west of the big city—we smoked a couple of joints. It was Saturday night and the club we always went to there was like a zoo. Balint got aggressively drunk at the bar, then picked out a group of six guys and got into it with them. He'd chosen them because there was no way we would win.

I hung my head and followed in the direction of the parking lot.

Registration

A pickup truck was speeding along the dirt road, its wheels beating up dust. It slowed, and came to a stop. Two men opened the doors and stepped out of the vehicle. They stood side by side off the road.

"You're not circumcised, huh?" said one. The man standing next to him, shorter by a head, finished up his business.

"No," he answered and zipped his pants. He took out a cigarette and lit up. The other man also finished urinating, and squinted into the setting sun.

"Hey, how far can you piss?"

"I don't know," said the stocky one. He thought about it. "A few yards." The weather had painted their blue fatigues gray. They both got back in the vehicle. They drove on in their white Mitsubishi, the bed in the back empty. In the cab, paper was scattered about and there was an empty cola bottle they used as an ashtray. From the rearview mirror hung a brown, plastic rosary that swung back and forth with the rhythm of the rocking vehicle. David was the name of the one asking questions. He sat in the passenger seat, fumbling with a white, three-ring binder. When he got tired of it he dropped the binder into his lap and turned to his companion.

"What does it feel like?"

"What does *what* feel like?" responded François, his English laden with a thick French accent. François clutched the wheel and watched the road.

"What else? What's it like to have a foreskin?"

"I don't know, what's the difference? If I had the chance, I would have had it removed," said François, turning on the headlights. The dirt road flashed brown in the beams of light.

"Why would you want to get it done?"

"What's it to you?"

"It's just that I don't know anybody with foreskin," said David, smirking. "So why?"

"Because I couldn't pull it back, that's why."

They went quiet for a bit; David fumbled with the binder, François watched the road. He looked over at the GPS by the wheel, checking where they were again. A red dot on the device showed the town's location, a place that three days before had been burned to the ground by the local militia. The government forces had since beaten the militia back over the border, and the roads were once again safe to travel. Seventy-two people from the town had been killed.

"I hate doing this now," grumbled François. "What's wrong with morning?"

"In the morning the delegation came," said David.

"And?"

"There needed to be a reception."

"I don't like going at night."

"We'll get it done in no time."

They stopped talking. David became absorbed in the NGO's special report. Nobody knew why the fighting had started. The

Dinka people who lived in the town were neutral parties in the war. Members of this small tribe were readily recognizable by the v-shaped scarring on their faces. There were scarcely two thousand in the entire country.

"I hope they buried them right this time," said François, and began to search for something on the radio.

"Yeah, the last time it stank to high heaven," David said, grinning at his French colleague's indignation.

"Right? It was fucking unbearable," said François. He gave up on finding a signal. They were too far from the base's transmission; only the noise of static filled the car.

"They should have shown *that* to the delegation," he grumbled as he turned off the radio. "The kind of stinking shit we work in."

David tried to imagine what the woman at the reception would have said about the previous village. Everybody had lined up to greet the guests, the entire staff, all forty of them. The commander gave a long speech as the guests sat in the shade drinking lemonade. A woman at lunch had complained to the commander about what strong smells there were in Africa. David could hardly contain his laughter when he overheard this. If not attended to in time, dead bodies would rot in days in the 108-degree heat.

François looked at the GPS, slowed, and turned off the road. They would have to continue on loose, grassy earth. David strained to look into the dusk. After a few minutes the remnants of huts appeared. The two gazed at the blackened walls against the horizon. François turned off the motor but left the headlights burning. He grabbed a camera from the back seat. David, binder in his hand, got out of the car.

"Let's start with the women. Were they separated?" asked François.

David flipped through the papers, plucked out a photocopied form, checked the information, and looked up.

"No. Everybody's together. Theoretically, the pit is two hundred yards north from the well."

"And where is the well?" asked François as he turned on his camera and checked the flash.

They stood looking around for a moment before David set off between the bullet-pocked hut remnants. After a brief search he found the well. It was a pit surrounded by mud bricks; a few steps away stood a trough. On the ground lay a leather sack with a long strap, which was fixed to a brick. The villagers used this to bring up the water. By the well were the tire tracks of the soldiers' jeeps. To shoot at the houses, they would have had to stop here. David stepped up to the well's perimeter. He took out his compass and checked the direction.

"That way," he said, pointing. They both started off. They beat their way through some bush, and continued on the white alkaline soil. The sun's last rays lit up the horizon, casting everything in the color of congealed blood.

"And what do women say, when they see you're not circumcised?" asked David as he lifted a few branches from their way. François stopped and took a cigarette from his pocket, lit up, and offered David the pack.

"Nothing. Usually nothing. Or, well, there was one . . . but she didn't really say anything," he said flatly.

"Then what did she *do*?" asked David and took a drag from his cigarette.

"She just pulled it back. She lifted it up and yanked the whole thing back," François demonstrated the action in the air.

"Did it rip? Was there blood?"

"So much that I thought I'd shit myself."

They both shuddered at the thought. Quiet fell on the bush.

Something was lying on the ground on the path in front of them. In the dusk they couldn't make out what it was, though they could smell decomposition. An unctuous odor filled the air.

"Goddamn it, if they left somebody here, I am not going farther," said François. He stopped and tried to make out the contours of the body lying in front of them. David went ahead to have a look. It was a donkey, its tongue hanging from the side of its mouth, its hide swarming with maggots. The body steamed in the cooling air. Cursing, François went after David. They gave the carrion a wide berth.

"Why isn't it with the rest?" asked François.

"They don't put the bodies of animals next to people," said David.

"Why not?"

"Beats me."

An oblong pit soon appeared before them. Next to it was a mound. The people who had dug the pit had obviously thrown the dirt there. Shovels were sticking out of the red soil, a sign the workers might be coming back. The two stepped to the edge. The pit was about a yard deep, and ten yards long. The black bodies had been carefully placed side by side along the bottom. David began to count, but soon lost track. François took pictures.

Using the flash, they saw that the people had been laid in the ditch with no regard for age: women, men, old, and young alike. Their clothing was soaked through with blood and their bodies had begun to decay in the equatorial weather. Despite this it could still be seen that the men had been killed with bullets, while the rest had been murdered with bayonets and rifle butts. They knew this because only the men's heads showed no wounds. The two stood quietly for a little while.

"Is it possible you didn't fuck the coordinator like last time?" said François and spat on the ground. David grimaced, and then began to take notes.

"Now is it seventy or seventy-two?" He looked questioningly at François.

"I don't know. I didn't count."

"Then count."

"Count my cock. What's the difference, if it's plus or minus a few? Write seventy."

The case number was already printed on the form. Only the geographical coordinates, the number of victims, and the name of the village needed to be filled in. David took out a pen and wrote in the number, then scratched his head with the pen.

"What was the reason?"

"For what?"

"For the killings."

"How should I know? Obviously the soldiers had something to do with it."

"Obviously," said David, staring into the ditch. "It's also possible that the villagers started it."

"Do these look like people who play rough?" grumbled François and spat into the pit.

"Aren't you just a little interested in what happened here?" asked David, unclipping a pocket light from his belt and shining it into the ditch.

"Write whatever you want," said François, and he resumed taking pictures.

David finished filling out the form. In the "Cause" line he wrote "Unknown," then shined the light into the pit again. There he noticed the untouched body of a girl. She was young, perhaps fifteen. Her left breast had fallen from her dress, and a man's hand rested on her stomach. Her face showed no wounds. They must have stabbed her from behind.

"Look how beautiful she was," he said, bending over the pit. "There isn't even any tribal scarring on her," he added.

François also looked into the ditch, and then began to smirk. He stood and with a stick pushed away the man's hand, so as to take in her whole body.

"So like the women in Abéché," said David.

"How do you know? You didn't come with us once."

"Of course not. They'll rot your cock off."

"The little Jew is touchy about his circumcised cock."

"I'm not touchy. I just heard that last year they cut somebody's whole prick off because he got some kind of infection."

"Bullshit. Nothing like that happened," said François and lit a cigarette. David also took one and lit up.

"I'm only saying. In the end the dude couldn't even walk. Some name starting with an "R": Ronald or Robert. An Irish radioman. I heard about it in the canteen."

"The Irish are Catholics. They don't even cut off their foreskins," said François, grinning.

"Cutting off the foreskin is beside the point here. If you stick it in a rotten place, it goes rotten. Supposedly the guy swelled up like a billy club. And it was all cheesed over."

"The girls in Abéché are clean."

"Like hell. They all have AIDS."

"You need to fuck with a condom."

"Yeah right, the Chinese ones don't fit my wang," said David, indicating the size with his hand.

"Mao Tse-tung had a little pecker," François said and began to guffaw.

They both laughed, then tossed their cigarette butts into the pit and began back to the truck.

"You just gotta get a blowjob, then there won't be any worries," said François. They walked around the rotting donkey and to the end of the village.

"That's all you gotta do."

They got in the car and pulled out onto the main road. François looked for music on the radio, but again found nothing. David threw the papers into the back and looked into the swarm of bugs, which had been attracted by the headlights.

"It is better to be circumcised, you know," said François.

"Yeah, and it's not just the Jews who do it. So do Christians. For the sake of hygiene."

"And it doesn't get cheesy if you miss a shower."

"No," David affirmed.

"And it's not as sensitive," said François.

"Why, is yours sensitive?"

"More sensitive than if they'd cut the skin from it."

"That's crap."

"It's not crap. It doesn't rub as much."

"So, because I am a Jew, my cock isn't sensitive enough."

"Yep."

"Then how sensitive is yours?"

"Very. And it has skin, so the cock is protected."

"That is so girly," laughed David, then added, "So you've got a touchy-feely cock."

"Exactly," grumbled François. "Now go suck your mother."

"How sensitive are you on a scale from one to ten?"

"Seven."

"That's pretty sensitive."

"That's what I'm saying."

"Why don't you just have it done?"

"No."

"Why, are you afraid you'll look like a Jew?"

"I'm just not letting anybody near it with a knife."

"That's fair. I wouldn't, either."

David sat back in the seat, put the binder in his lap, and finished filling in the information. He just wasn't sure about the village's name. But François remembered from the canteen: it had been written with a magic marker in the daily work schedule. It was called Darhu. David managed to write it correctly on the second try.

End of the World

If you decide that you want to see the end of the world, you will need the permission of the military in Sana'a. The night will be heavy and cold. No more so than in Europe, perhaps, but there won't be electricity and you can see the stars. You will be up in the hills, in the middle of a crater, where they built a city near the sky.

You were always curious about the end of the world. The zero point where everything reaches its end. Civilization, culture, government, order—everything. All the rules that bind the world. Unlike the center of the world, you can go to the end of the world, because there's no competition to get there. Where questions of religion and discrimination can't find you.

They will summon you for 7:30 PM at headquarters, half an hour before evening prayer and twenty minutes before the khat begins to kick in in their hearts and heads. You know, because your mouth will also be filled with khat. You will swallow the bitter and green spit until the effect takes hold.

"True, its kiss is more bitter than a woman's, but it's a kiss of eternal pleasure," the dealer you buy it from says. He'll only cheat you by a few dollars, because he thinks you are Muslim when you slip in an Egyptian-accented "Salam."

You knock at headquarters, but you wait in vain for somebody to answer. With two fists you beat the door until someone finally opens up. It will be a conscript, a familiar-looking weapon in his hand and his cheeks stuffed with khat.

He will show off his small piece of Hungary. Since you set foot in the Middle East, you'd hoped that this wouldn't be how people know your homeland. You figured that even in the Gaza Strip they'd speak of soccer legend Ferenc Puskás, the Golden Team, or the Rubik's Cube. Anything but this. That a young Hamas recruit wouldn't tell you what a wonder the Automatic Modified Paratrooper rifle is, what a great people you are, because your country gave the world something you can properly kill with, and that it even comes with a scope mount. For a moment you hope that this won't happen, that the talk will be about Puskás, Rubik, the Golden Team, or even paprika—but no. You are Hungarian so it's the AMD-65 rifle. Slowly it dawns on you why every Hungarian embassy in the area has a military attaché. You can't spit because your mouth is full of dry khat.

The conscript will grin at you, strike the floor with green spit, then indicate that you should follow him. The corridor you walk down is lit by petroleum lamps, and it takes you past the weapon stockpile. The collection, which includes the Eastern Bloc's every last wonder, will be on a long, hardwood-carved lunch table.

He escorts you to a door, its red paint flaking. You enter; there sits an older soldier. In his eye you will see that he is *good with God*. He looks at you with childlike amazement. He doesn't understand what you are looking for in this country when they are killing your sort. With his hand he shows how five—exactly five—Westerners were killed by Al Qaeda just yesterday. To drive home his point he passes his finger across his neck. Yes, they cut their throats. You think of Marie, the flaxen-haired blonde with a Dutch accent whom you met at the hotel. You picture how they cut her throat.

You have seen it already in the method they use to kill chickens—if your line of work has taught you anything, it's that people aren't much different in death. God comes to your mind as well; you repeat in your mother tongue that he doesn't exist. That's why you will do this, because you are becoming increasingly unsure of this assertion. It only happened by chance that you didn't go with Marie, that you weren't killed as well.

You will smile at the officer because you have no better idea what to do. You say you don't want to leave the country, you would just like to ask permission to travel tomorrow, south to the sea, to Aden. He will ask what you want to do there. You lie and say that you are going to visit an NGO. You know you won't get permission if you tell them you are going to interview rebels.

"Did you bring me a gift?" the officer will ask, and you will put a hundred-dollar bill on the table. He smiles at you and signs your papers. "May the protector watch over you," he says and walks you to the entrance.

Outside, the night covers you. You are freezing and you will be able to see your breath, so you stumble back to the hotel. Somebody on the street will put a candle in your hand so you don't get lost.

You lie on the cot and listen to the roaches, how they appear when darkness descends on the room. You can't see anything, just the dark, and something moving. Then you feel the khat in your head, releasing you from the darkness, from the company of roaches. It lulls you until you are far away, so far.

You will wake at the call to morning prayer. It is cold. You will pack up your stuff; all that is important to you fits in just a backpack. You go to the mosque. The Muslims won't say anything, but whisper behind your back. The imam's voice will shake with emotion at the discovery that an infidel can also understand God's word.

When prayer is over you will ask directions to the bus station. Twenty men will escort you there. You ask why, and they say it is because you are all brothers.

You have difficulty extracting yourself from them, but eventually you are able to buy a ticket for Ta'izz. You begin to look for the bus and get lost among the vendors. From the hagglers you hear the daily news. Al Qaeda has announced that "they can no longer guarantee safety for foreigners in the country." Everybody is fleeing. The government is allowing multiple flights to depart from the airport on behalf of the trapped foreigners.

You find your bus from among the dozen waiting. Cages of chickens, luggage, and people sit on the roof, as with every other bus at the station. When one of the buses departs, feathers drift down through the swirling air.

You try to board. The driver, a fiftyish man, gives a start when he sees you. He jumps from behind the wheel, grabs your shoulder, and begins to plead with you not to choose his bus. From his wallet, he shows you pictures of his children. He grovels, saying he doesn't want you to travel with him, because anything could happen, and your protection would be his responsibility. If you get robbed or shot, if you were to disappear, he would be taken in front of the authorities; he would be sentenced to ten years' hard labor for taking part in a terrorist act.

You have no cause to argue. You will just stand there, focused on the pleading driver, who goes on to explain how in your Western clothing you would stick out in the crowd like a bone in sand; only an idiot wouldn't notice you. You could dress in a jellabiya, and you can stick a *jambiya* in your belt, but it would be pointless because you can't change your hair or eye color. You are about to give up when somebody from the mosque appears.

You realize that a heated argument has broken out over you. It is put to the driver that he should take you, lest he get struck down by the archangel Gabriel himself for not helping one of God's pale but elected children. You never get involved in religious arguments. You just don't speak, because you already know it would be pointless.

Since you set foot in the Middle East, you have been able to explain everything about yourself, outside of your relationship with God. You can say where you came from and what you are doing, you can buy chicken or rabbit, but not that you don't believe in God. Everything but that.

You once tried to explain to a taxi driver in Cairo, when asked about your religion, that you are not Muslim, you are not Christian, you aren't anything. "Bidun Allah," you said by way of explanation. He looked at you, nodded, and said he had no problem with the Jews. This is how you came to understand that in the Middle East, atheism just doesn't exist. If you say to an Arab that you are "without God," it means you are a Jew.

The argument will result with you being let on the bus as a Muslim brother who has to be watched out for. You will find a spot between a woman who smells of sweat and a goatherd. In front of you sit some Palestinians. You will see their wounds and know that they are the fleeing opposition. Their wounds are material reminders of their resistance to political Islam.

The bus starts up, the driver looking worriedly into the rearview mirror. He's keeping an eye on you. You leave the town behind and ride along a curvy, rocky road. You look out the window: the ground is red and the sky is near, as if you are traveling on Mars; patches of khat and shot-up armored vehicles are the only reminders that people live here.

Halfway to Ta'izz you will have to cross a military checkpoint. The bus will need to wait an hour while you are being interviewed. The soldier wants to make clear that you are crazy to travel at this time; but when he sees he can't talk you out of it, that you are determined to see the end of the world, he tucks half a kilo of khat into your jacket pocket. "At least you will feel good. Just don't get off the bus unless it's necessary."

Of course at the first occasion you disobey the command and disembark with the rest of the passengers at a stop in front of a restaurant. There will be a well near the building, and you will watch the sheep take water while you eat. Lepers come to beg, but the restaurant owner chases them off with a stick. The cement is sprinkled with their blood.

Five men from the bus stay at your side so you don't get into trouble. Volunteers. With Argos eyes they examine every approaching figure, their hands on their jambiyas, blades half drawn. In places like this the tribes frequently take high-value hostages. And with your white skin you are an obvious target.

Before the turnoff for Ta'izz, you tell the driver you want to get off. When you cut through the crowd of passengers, two suggest they accompany you to be on the safe side. You summon up your best Arabic to thank them. You do so in the Muslim fashion, so as to calm them. If you say it like this, they will believe that you are indeed blessed and angels sit on your shoulder, and that *peace will be with you.* They will believe, because unlike in your country, in this land spoken words have magic.

You get off and watch the huge dust cloud kicked up by the Ta'izz-bound bus. The passengers wave good-bye from the windows. When the bus finally disappears in the distance you look around. You will see a red rocky landscape and sparsely growing shrubbery; your shirt sticks to your skin. You are not in the hills anymore.

You wait for around twenty minutes, but no ride comes. Your mouth is dry. You curse yourself that you didn't bring water.

An hour passes. Your limbs start to cramp from dehydration and you wonder how long you can last like this, here in the middle of nowhere. Just when you've accepted that you will be spending the night in the desert, a small goat appears.

At first the goatherd mistakes you for an evil spirit wandering among the rocks. In the ensuing conversation it is all you can do to convince him that you are not evil. He points his Kalashnikov at you (you recognize it as one made back home) and shouts at you until you say the Shahada. Once you have convinced him that you are a Muslim, he lowers the gun and offers you some goat milk. He asks where you are headed. You say the end of the world. He nods and informs you that the place is 150 kilometers from where you are standing. And beyond the end of the world begins darkness, the place of weeping and gnashing of teeth.

While you talk, you let him touch your skin. He has never seen such white skin up close, and he still suspects you are not a real person. You offer him khat in exchange for the goat milk. You both sit and chew. His tribe lives only six miles from here, and if you decide you want company, he can take you to the end of the world in their only car. You accept.

You and the goatherd walk the six miles through the darkening desert. After night has fallen and the giant swelling moon bathes everything in light, the huts appear.

Everybody comes out to stare at you until the men order the women and children back inside. A gray-haired elder, the *qadi,* steps up to you. When you say that you are Hungarian, he nods. There is such a country; you can see relief on his face.

The qadi invites you into his hut and offers you meat. He promises that tomorrow they will take you to Aden, if you really want to see the end of the world. He asks only that you eat with him now. The meal with the elder takes around two hours, after which you lie down on a rug he lays out for you. There you will sleep while the qadi's wives and children eat the leftovers.

Arthur Rimbaud wrote of Aden: "This is a stinking cesspool, the end of the world." A plaque at your hotel commemorates the fact that the poet embarked upon his African career from here, though they spell his name wrong.

You bid the tribesmen good-bye and get a room at the hotel. You can barely breathe because the sea air is so heavy.

You do the work you have here, but all the while you are thinking of the end of the world, and wondering just what street it's on. You rove about carelessly at night, and after somebody punches you out and takes your cell phone and two hundred dollars, your mouth will be salty with blood.

You can't find the end of the world anywhere, just old colonialist buildings, heat, and the smell of disease. And right when you are about to give up, you find it.

The end of the world can indeed be found in Aden, in the brothel named The Sailor's Club, the only place in the city where they serve alcohol. Built on a pier, practically sitting in the sea.

At the door, they look askew at your bloody shirt, but you are white, so they let you in. You will tap your ring against your beer to signal to the girls: yes to another drink, but nothing more. But of course you don't run away when one of the black girls sits next to you. "Special prices," she will say, and you will refer to her as "Jasmine" later, because you are too ashamed to ask her name.

You ask her where she comes from to steer the conversation away from business. "From there," she says and points toward the sea into the darkness.

"This here is the end of the world. Here the rules no longer apply. In this place, in this bar," you put to her when she stands up from the table.

"My home fell from the earth long ago," she says, and moves to the table of another man.

You will sit alone in the bar for a long time, staring into the darkness. Rifle fire flashes in the distance, beyond where the waters of Somalia begin.

Twins

We snaked our way through the hills. The grass sprouted in clumps along the slopes, the sand revealing itself in patches; only from a distance did it all seem to blend together. It was eight in the morning, and a cool breeze blew off the desert, the juniper bushes shining with dew. Sheep grazed in the distance, and we could hear the sound of the bells that the rams wore from their necks. After driving past abandoned, shot-up tanks and the desert itself, Libya's green hills were a welcome sight.

"Do you think they will attack today?" I asked Hamid. He blinked as the sun hit his eyes. I rolled the window down and took two cigarettes from the pack. The air was already tepid, promising a sweltering noon. I lit both cigarettes and handed one to him.

"*Inshallah*," he said, and took a long drag. "If NATO gives the green light, then we commence."

"It's already been a week with no action. They're just taking potshots at each other."

"True. You see, Gaddafi's men have learned to be sneaky. They fly the same flags as us on their cars, so NATO can't tell the difference. But we will attack when NATO gives the word that they have taken out their rocket launchers."

The mere mention of the rocket launchers was enough for me to hear the scream of the Grad rockets in my head and the thundering noise of exploding shells. For two weeks now I had been listening for their sound on the Ajdabiya front. The advancing Gaddafi soldiers always attacked the lines of the rebels early in the morning, during prayer. They weren't able to aim the rockets precisely, and whenever they managed to hit, the destruction was massive.

"Nobody knows when the blitz will be?"

"Allah Karim, Abu Abdel Hafiz! Only the Transitional Council knows. At least I hope somebody knows when this wretched offensive will be!"

I knew Hamid's outburst wasn't directed at me. His boy was stationed at Ajdabiya with a group of insurgents, and he would take part in the fight for Brega once the offensive began. Brega was a meat grinder. In a civil war with no end in sight, it had already changed hands four times.

We puffed our cigarettes in silence. I fixed my gaze on Hamid's face. It was wrinkled with worry. He was just fifty, but he appeared much older when the thought of his son crossed his mind. Then the wrinkles creased deeper across his face: out of worry for their boys, fathers all over Libya were aging like this. Before the uprising, Hamid had been a doctor, but with his good English, he became a driver to foreign journalists during the conflict, along with serving on the Transitional Council. We had met in Benghazi, quite by accident, after the rocket bombardments.

"I apologize that I can't take you directly to Tobruk, Abu Abdel Hafiz," he said, regaining his composure. He had been calling me Abu Abdel Hafiz since I told him that I had named my son Hafiz. We had been sitting in his car when Gaddafi's sharp-shooters began to fire on us in Ajdabiya, and it was then that we became friends. People bond easier in war. Nobody wants to die next to a stranger.

"As long as you take me, no problem. I'm not rushing anywhere. And don't worry about your boy. It will be alright."

"Inshallah. But if he dies, it will be for a just cause. God loves his martyrs."

"But you don't want him to die, do you?"

"Of course not. I am his father. But God's ways are unfathomable. If God wills it, he will die as a martyr, and of course I also fear this."

We turned off the paved road. The earth was red and damp, and the sun was so blindingly bright we could hardly see the ruins of Cyrene. The sunshine spilled from the hills and onto the ancient statues, columns, and ruined stone houses.

"We are going to Shahat, it's close now," said Hamid. "You can see a shahid burial."

"One of your relatives?"

"No. They asked me to make an entrance in the register of the dead before the burial. I am a doctor, so it is something I can do."

"Where are the doctors of the town?"

"At the front, like all the other men. Just the old and wounded stayed behind."

"Why do you need a registry of the dead?"

"Because if we prevail, the new government will remember the martyrs of the revolution. Having the paperwork will help."

At the checkpoint where the street began, the guards recognized Hamid's car and waved us on. We drove between the whitewashed houses and pulled up in front of a two-story house. In the yard stood a tent made of dark linen. From speakers rose the sound of devotional music. In front of the tent stood an older, gray-haired man. Next to him was a young man of perhaps twenty.

"Let's go and congratulate the father," said Hamid, killing the ignition.

"Won't I be disturbing him?"

"Of course not! You are bringing the news of his son to the world."

The tent was almost full with people sitting on plastic chairs. A picture was positioned in the front: a portrait of the martyr, I guessed, though I couldn't make it out so well. Two men stepped up to the tent before us, but before they went in, each clasped the old man's hand and said, "Congratulations on your son."

"Ahmed Bakush, your son is already with the angels," said Hamid in Arabic, when we made it to the tent.

"Alhamdulillah," answered the old man. "It is a great honor for us."

He held his hand out to me. "You must be the journalist. *Ahlen.*"

"Thanks," I said, taking his hand and shaking it, then involuntarily offering my hand to the young man as well.

"Khalid Bakush," said the boy. He stood there looking downcast, his eyes red with sleeplessness. He had short black hair, his skin was light brown, and his eyes were also brown. He was striking, most certainly well liked among the local women.

"You can be proud of your brother, Khalid. Pray that God grants you as much courage as he had," said Hamid, turning to the boy.

"Yes, I am proud," came the choked response as the boy hung his head.

"Where is the Shahid?" asked Hamid.

"Inside. Hurry, we are waiting for you to begin the burial," said the older man.

"Okay, but we can't stay for the ceremony. We have to get back to Tobruk and find a car to Salloum."

More pallbearers arrived. Hamid went back to the car and retrieved his attaché case from the trunk.

"Can I go in with you?" I asked as we made our way to the house.

"Come, if you want."

Hamid knocked loudly to signal we were entering and that the women should clear out. The inside of the house was set in gloom, the shades drawn tight. A tile stairway led to the upper level. After a search in the darkness, Hamid found the lamp.

It was a sparsely furnished room, with three mattresses centered on a Persian carpet. The boy was laid out on one of them. He couldn't have been more than twenty years old, his body torn and bloodied in fatigues that looked gritted over with sand. His skin was gray, as if he had been dead for days. His eyes were closed. I stood speechless at the door. The boy was a spitting image of the one whom I had met outside the tent.

"You didn't mention they were twins."

"Indeed, they are. Muhammad was older by just a few minutes. Both are nineteen. Now please give me a hand."

"What are we going to do?"

"Undress him and examine the wounds."

Hamid stepped up to the corpse, knelt beside it on the rug, and began to unbutton his fatigues. The boy's face was dirty, and his skin and hair were encrusted with sand.

"Don't think the parents are barbarians because they didn't wash or change their martyr's clothing," said Hamid. He finally finished unbuttoning the jacket, the material coming unstuck from the wounds with a smacking sound. The ripe stench of congealed blood wafted across the room. The boy's chest was bullet-pocked and smeared with blood.

"In accordance with the Hadith, the shahid gets buried in the same place and in the same clothing in which his life was taken," he said. With clinical eyes he looked over the boy's chest. He opened his attaché case and withdrew a form and a fountain pen. He touched the tip of the pen to one of the bullet wounds. I counted three small red craters, each capped with blood.

"Yes, it's a 7.62 size round," said Hamid.

"How do you know?"

"The tip of my pen is the same size as a 7.62 round. This is the entrance wound. If you compare it to the pen, you can establish what kind of bullet it was. If the wound is smaller than the pen, then a 9 mm shot was used, something like a pistol or machine gun. If bigger, then a 50 was used. It must be said that if you find a 50, you won't have to measure it, because the body will be ripped apart. A 50 really tears apart the body. I do it this way because in Islam, it is a sin to cut up a martyr. The pen method is the only way we can establish just how he met his end."

He began to fill out the form.

"The paper concerning his internal organs, I won't bother with," he said.

"Do you know how it happened?" I asked.

"Three days earlier there was a tank attack by Gaddafi's men in Brega. Muhammad and his group took to a ditch while the tanks advanced toward the city. According to Khalid's account, they lay petrified in the ditch because the tank had spotted them and began to fire. Nobody made a move except for Muhammad. It is obvious that between the two brothers, he was the more courageous. Now help me turn him over, please."

We stood, lifted the corpse, and turned him on to his stomach. The body was stiff. The shirt was just tatters on his back; the rounds had torn his skin to shreds where the bullet had exited. Hamid began to write again.

"And?"

"Well, the wounds definitely show that Muhammad fought like a true mujahid. They only had one RPG; he jumped up and shot it at the tank, taking out its wheels. The tank returned fire, of course, but by then the others had already retreated."

"He might have lived if he had been wearing a vest."

"The mujahideen don't wear them."

"Why not?"

"It slows them down."

"That's stupid."

"It's not stupid. A bulletproof vest weighs thirty pounds. Plus, every mujahideen hopes to be taken by God."

"And because of this they are willing to do stupid things?"

"No. Just willing to make sacrifices."

"Why?"

"Because the Prophet, peace be upon him, taught us that he who makes a sacrifice for the just cause and loses his life will go immediately to Paradise."

"Were both brothers mujahideen?"

"Yes. They both asked their father to allow them to follow the call of the Jihad. Muhammad was the more fortunate. He is already with God. Khalid brought the body home. He didn't stop at the Ajdabiya front, but came straight here."

"But you said before that he should be buried where he fell."

"Yes, but it's not so strict. It is more important that we hold the ground. If Gaddafi's soldiers break through again, they will desecrate the graves. That's why Khalid brought the body home. Now help me turn him back."

We flipped the body over. It wasn't an easy job to dress him again, because the buttons were slippery with blood.

"It's a big honor for their family. Ahmed Bakush should be very proud of his older boy. The whole of Libya should be as

well. He lived and died according to Islam. Come on, let's wash
our hands."

We stood and headed downstairs. The sink was on the
ground floor.

"Now what will happen?"

"Now the men will come in. They'll sew him into white
linen, and carry him on their shoulders to the graveyard. There is
already an open grave waiting. We needn't stick around for this,
because we should get to Tobruk before sundown, and you need
to find a car going to Salloum."

As I was washing with lavender-smelling soap, I heard shouting
coming from outside. We went to the door. A large crowd stood
on the street, the men shaking their fists in the air. A few people
in the crowd began to shove and push, and the women in the
procession wailed loudly.

"Get in the car and wait," said Hamid, putting the key in
my hand. I sat in the car and watched Hamid disappear into the
crowd. I turned on the radio. The patriotic songs of Free Libya
murmured forth, and then the Transitional Council's spokesper-
son came on and announced that the revolutionary army's offensive to retake Brega had begun; currently the rebels were engaged
in fighting in the city's outer districts. It was a quarter hour before Hamid returned, walking to the car with quick footsteps. He
opened the door and sat.

"Okay, let's go," said Hamid, turning off the radio. Hamid
gave the car some gas, and the wheels began to turn. We left the
crowd behind and drove away, turning past the checkpoint to the
main road. We drove for a while in silence. He looked somehow
pained.

"What was the commotion out there?" I asked, finally
breaking the quiet.

"Khalid, the younger brother, shot himself."

"What?"

"Yes, he did. It's the most disgusting sin. You go to hell for it."

"Does this happen often?"

"Not at all. It is forbidden in Islam."

We were back on the serpentine main road. The sun was blazing by now and the air was balmy. Above us, Cyrene's ancient rocks shone on the hillside like white teeth in a skull.

Somewhere on the Border

The Gaza border crossing was out in the desert. Low brown hills rose on the horizon, the air above them appearing to quiver with the wind-blown sands. On the Palestinian side there stood a lone café, built with one side open. People went there to escape the heat.

It was summer. It had been sweltering and dry in the city, but the desert was even hotter. More than a hundred people were waiting to cross the border into Egypt. The café's one plastic table couldn't accommodate everybody, so those who didn't get a seat leaned against the bullet-ridden wall, waiting, listlessly watching the grimy ceiling fan churning the hot air.

I sat at the table inside with Marwan. I had already been waiting sixteen hours for them to open the border so I could return to Egypt. Because of the blockade, things like this were a bureaucratic nightmare.

For six years now Israel had kept the Gaza Strip under closure by land, water, and air. The only reason there wasn't famine was because hundreds of tunnels ran under the border, through which goods from Egypt were smuggled in. The trip through a tunnel lasted an hour, cost a hundred dollars, and you could die there if a rocket from Israel landed. But the legal route was time consuming; nobody was surprised if they had to wait four or five days.

"Another coffee?" I asked Marwan and set the empty plastic bottle I had been playing with back on the table.

"We can have another."

"*Itnen ahwa sadaa*," I called out to the waiter, who nodded, then shuffled back to the unit's grimy kitchen. I marveled at how dirty his feet were. But in the café everything was filthy, myself included. It was because of the dust, the fine desert sand in the air. It stuck to your skin and mixed with your sweat to darken your clothing. Marwan was watching the crowd gather by the steel gate. They solemnly pleaded with machine-gun-toting Hamas soldiers, but the gates weren't being opened for anybody.

"You know, I was thinking, you don't really speak Arabic," said Marwan.

"Then what do I speak?"

"Egyptian."

"So what's the problem?"

"It's not a problem. It's just not Arabic."

"Of course it's Arabic. There are only minor phonetic differences."

"Then it's not Arabic. Palestinian isn't real Arabic either."

"So what is real Arabic?"

"The Koran. That's Arabic. The rest are just dialects."

The waiter brought our coffee and set it on the table, along with small glasses of water. Bits of rust were floating in the water. Without a thought, Marwan tossed his back, and then lit a cigarette.

"The Hamas officer said he would come here with your passport to tell you when you can cross."

"Great."

"Did you hide the cassettes?"

"Yep. They're in my underwear."

"Good. They won't frisk you, don't worry."

"I'm not worried."

"It's good material, right? I mean, it's worth a lot of money."

"Yes, it's good material."

I leaned back in my chair. I was beginning to sweat through my shirt. I felt the cassettes pressing against my skin. On the tapes men told of how family members of the Hamas government were being maimed or killed.

It really was good material, and we had worked hard to get it. Marwan had arranged all the interviews in secret, under the cover of night. He worked with striking resolve, fearlessly. If we messed up, Hamas would execute him without a second thought. I pulled out a cigarette and lit up, the smoke feeling no hotter than the air.

"This is the worst, this waiting," I said.

"We can always take the tunnels. Then you can say in Egypt that you lost your passport. That way we can go together."

"I thought we talked about this, Marwan. I can't go by the tunnel, because I didn't come by the tunnel. I can't risk it if they turn me away in Egypt."

"I know, but I'll miss you, brother."

"One week, Marwan. It's nothing. I will speak with the consul, who will write a letter that will get you permission to leave. Then I'll come pick you up in Arish."

"And if he doesn't send the letter?"

"He will. He's a friend of mine."

"It would be better to go with you."

"It would make me happier too, but it's not possible. You just need to wait a week. Then we will go together and you will work for me as my cameraman. We'll see the Sudanese refugee camps. We'll earn tons of money."

"I don't care about money."

"I know."

"I just want to go with you from this godforsaken Gaza. It's the devil's paradise. Cross the border and wait at Rafah. I'll take the tunnel. Then we will go together to Cairo."

"And what will you do without papers? You'll be shipped right back." I said this louder than I should have. The others at our table turned toward us. "One week, Marwan. Just a week," I continued, more quietly. "But we've already been over this."

"Okay. I'll stay and keep my head down."

"You said there wouldn't be trouble. If there will be trouble, I won't leave you here."

"Hamas will definitely want to talk with me, because they knew I was with you."

"So what will you do?"

"I'll stay out of sight with my relatives in Khan Yunis. It's no problem as long as the tapes aren't played on TV while I'm here. They won't be, right?"

"Of course not."

"And you'll come back in a week? No matter what, you will come, right?"

"We already discussed this. I'll come get you in a week. I don't know why we are talking about this again."

"Don't be angry. It's because of the heat. It makes a person nervous. Shall we drink something, brother?"

"No, I've had enough of this café already."

"I'll bring a water."

"Fine."

He stood and went to the rear part of the café, where the waiter was setting drinks on a tray. Sweat broke out on my brow and dripped into my eyes. I took out a tissue and wiped my face. I thought about how every conflict is the same, how the regions may change, but the way you spend your time is always the same.

This is what war's about: waiting. You wait for something to happen. You wait in a hotel room, in a café, you wait on the front line, by the fire of a camp, and you do all this as though you have a chance of understanding what is going on. But you don't. If something does happen, it happens too fast for you to get it. The only thing you understand is that you are waiting again. That's your work, to convey the private hell of others, as though you understand it or as though it has anything to do with you.

Marwan returned to the table, a bottle of mineral water in his hand. He sat and poured a glass.

"Look," he said, and gestured toward the entrance. A black BMW had pulled up in front of the café, reflecting everything in its tinted windows. The door opened and a thirty-something balding man emerged, dressed in an Armani suit and patent leather shoes. He was a surreal sight in these filthy surroundings.

"Look. That one's a killer."

"Why do you think?"

"Just watch."

The waiter rushed out when he saw the man. We couldn't hear what they were saying, but the guy must have ordered something, because the waiter hurried back to the fridge and retrieved a bottle of water.

"He won't have to wait," said Marwan. "Hamas's killers don't need to wait for anything."

"Again, why do you think he's a killer?"

"Only killers have such eyes. Look at his expression. Their eyes are like this, like glass."

"I don't see anything. How do you figure?"

"I am Palestinian. I've known a killer or two."

I looked the man over, but didn't see anything unusual about his face. His eyes were olive-green and bored. I couldn't imagine him, in his elegant suit, shooting somebody in the leg—not the way they usually did it in the Gaza Strip. If they thought you had loose lips, they would find you at night, press the rifle barrel into your leg, and shoot so the bullet blows the leg bone to pieces and comes out the heel. Nobody can stand on a shattered leg bone; the limb is generally amputated from the knee down. They would also push people from rooftops. Sometimes it happened that they didn't have to push; it was enough to remind men that they had wives and children, and the men would jump themselves. Those were the things we covered in the interviews over the past few days; those were the stories I was taking with me in my underwear.

"I should have been a killer," said Marwan. "I'd have been a good one, don't you think?"

"No, I don't think you'd have been a good one. You're too sensitive."

"This is true. But I should have at least given it a try."

"Don't talk crap. Of course you shouldn't have tried. You're too smart to be a killer."

"That doesn't matter. Whatever happened, I'd live better than most. It's just my eyes. I'd be sorry for my eyes."

The waiter brought the water for the man in the suit; the man paid him, then got back into his car and drove off. The soldiers pushed the crowd back with their rifles and held the gate open for the car. The whole scene lasted no more than five minutes.

"See? What did I say? Killers don't need to wait."

"It's also possible he's a politician or diplomat."

"He was a killer, I'm telling you. Give me a cigarette, please. I'm out."

I passed him the pack. Marwan took one and lit up. From outside came the din of the crowd of people pleading to be let through. We didn't speak; we just watched a family weighed down with luggage and wailing children. A few minutes later a black-clad Hamas soldier entered the café. The long black beard that hung from his face collected drops of sweat and appeared to sparkle in the sun.

"Foreigner!" he shouted.

"That's you," Marwan said, signaling the soldier, who stepped up to our table.

"Here is your passport, foreigner. You can cross. Your permission arrived from Egypt. Follow me."

We stood up from the table, made our way through the crowd, and then walked down the dirt road to the gate. The soldier opened it a crack, and we stepped through. A booth stood by the chain-link fence. The bearded soldier gave the man inside my passport so he could take down my information.

"Have a great trip, brother," said Marwan, hugging me. "You're coming back for sure?"

"Definitely."

"Good. I will wait for you every day. Just a week?"

"Yes. Just a week."

I got my passport back and took a taxi to the Egyptian side. The border crossing there was empty, so I didn't have to wait to get my stamp. After making it over the border I haggled with a Bedouin to take me to Cairo. He drove me in his beat-up Mercedes truck. I sat in the passenger seat. The horizon was brown; a storm was brewing above the desert.

I spent a long time gazing into the rearview mirror, studying my eyes. They were the same as always.

Homecoming

They were there to hunt deer. The young man's father had arranged the paperwork with the hunting association, giving them permission to shoot a few animals. Dusk found them already in the forest's easternmost region. His father and the father's friend had brought the rifles; the young man had recently returned from Africa, and didn't have one of his own. The fading sun shone through the leaves as they made their way to the wooden tower blinds. They had unpacked the equipment from the car, which they'd parked by the cabin. There was still a month left in summer and the blueberries by the path were ripe.

The father handed the rifle to his son, saying only, "The Remington 7 is yours." The young man took it wordlessly and checked the bolt. It was a high-caliber weapon with a walnut stock, loaded with the type of expanding, dum-dum bullet his dad used for wild boars. For shooting a deer, his father's favorite rifle, an antique Mauser, would have been enough. His grandfather had found it in the forest, where it lay discarded by a fleeing

German soldier. Between them they'd kept the weapon hidden for fifty years.

"We can still have a smoke here," said the father's friend, and passed around a pack of Marlboros. The young man looked into the face of his father, the man whom the doctor had forbidden from smoking. All three took a cigarette and lit up.

"Don't tell your mother. You know what she's like," said the father, turning to him.

"What's she like?" interjected the father's friend.

"Well, she worries."

"Why, what's the problem?"

"I have high blood pressure. High risk of a heart attack."

"But you didn't actually *have* a heart attack."

"No," said the father and stubbed his cigarette out against a tree trunk.

"Then why worry?"

"Well, you know what she's like."

They went farther down the path, hazelnut and oak trees lining the way. Dark was falling fast: minute by minute the shadows grew and the animals ventured farther from cover. The birds went quiet in the trees, and only a few crickets could be heard. They were already close to the clearing where the tower blinds were. They took their rifles from their shoulders and loaded them. The son pointed the barrel at the ground; he didn't need his father to remind him of anything about hunting.

"And what was it like in Africa?" the father's friend asked the son. "You've become awful quiet."

"It was good."

"Where were you exactly?"

"Sudan."

"Isn't there a war there?"

"Yeah."

The father, panting now, stopped to catch his breath. They all stopped.

"I'm proud of you," he said to the young man and leaned against a tree.

"You should be," said the father's friend. "Not just anybody can go photograph a war."

The young man didn't say a thing; he just gazed at his father's boots in the dark. The old man had aged over the past year. His belly stuck out and he had become frail. The mother and her son frequently joked about this, if only to ease the simple sorrow of the fact. "We've become antique porcelain dolls," they'd said to him when he got off the train. The father had looked down at his boots when he saw his son's expression of surprise.

"What is it?"

"Nothing."

They arrived at the clearing, its two tower blinds appearing at opposite edges. Grass had grown over the tree stumps that marked where the forest once stood. In neighboring Austria, the wood brought a good price. A tree disease spreading through the forest was a good enough pretext for chopping it down, and in turn keeping the hunting association's till full. This had happened years ago, before the appearance of Italian guest hunters. Since then, they had no need to sell the trees. In the countryside, boars and all kinds of other game could be found, attracting foreign hunters in droves. A living could be made from it.

When they arrived at the edge of the clearing, the father began to speak. The crickets chirped in the grass.

"We can't leave behind any animal we've wounded, because it will die in agony."

"Of course, of course," said the father's friend. "But we've been hunting together for ten years now. Do you need to say this every time?"

"It was something I heard from my father," the old man said, looking into the son's face.

"I'm more interested in hearing how Africa was."

"The weather was nice," said the son.

"Tell us about it in the cabin. We'll be here for two more weeks," said the father. "Now let's climb up the towers. We'll go up this one, as usual. The other one's yours," he said, turning to his son.

The question posed by his father's friend echoed in the young man's head as he trod toward the tower. He climbed the ladder and sat on the perch. The moon appeared from behind the clouds, illuminating the clearing. He saw the tower opposite, embers flashing from cigarettes the father and his friend were smoking. It was a full moon, but not as bright as it would have been in the desert.

"Do you love me?" Rania had asked him in Khartoum, as she ran her hand along his chest. "Because I love you very much." The woman's white teeth flashed as she broke into laughter, black laughter. "You're an ugly white," she said, "but your eyes are blue and green. Green after lovemaking."

The young man gazed at Rania as she combed her hair in the mirror. He liked to look at her back and how she worked the comb through her hair. "You are like a gazelle," he said, stepping up to the mirror so he could touch her. "Light a cigarette for me," said the girl, leaning forward so as to touch his hand. He lit the cigarette. Rania stood from the seat and kissed him on the lips. During the kiss he blew smoke into her mouth. "Gypsy kiss," said the young man. "That's what it's called in my country."

The wind began to blow from the east. The young man leaned out of the tower but saw only the bushes rustling in the wind.

He could just make out snatches of conversation from the other tower: the father and his friend were talking about the state of the country's national soccer teams, and both were swearing. The young man thought how nice it would be to light a cigarette and drink a beer. There was a case waiting for them back at the cabin, if only his father would call off the hunt. As he looked up at the moon, the terrace of the Carlton Hilton popped into his mind.

"You won't leave me on my own. I slept with you and this brings shame on me as a Muslim girl."

"You're not a real Muslim," said the young man. "And you weren't a virgin."

They both worked for a humanitarian foundation and were paid in hard currency. Whereas the young man photographed the refugee camps and the genocide, Rania was the local interpreter, speaking four languages fluently. When he flew home, she'd accompanied him to the airport in tears. She sent a few letters to him, but when she got no response, she gave up.

Something moved in the brush. At first the young man thought it was the wind, but after a few moments it became clear that an animal was coming his way. It couldn't have been too big; from the sound he concluded that it was probably a fawn. He raised his gun to his shoulder and waited. He hoped that the animal would change its mind and not step into the clearing, because he didn't want to kill it. He waited through a few quiet minutes. He was thinking he had gotten lucky, and then the deer appeared. It was a young one, beautiful and muscular. He aimed at the heart. As he put his finger on the trigger, the email from that morning returned to him.

"The people who carried out the coup are closing all bank accounts. I can't get my money. At any moment they could invalidate my passport. They have already slaughtered five members of my family and they even shot my father. Please send money so I can get out of here. Five hundred euros for a ticket to Paris. You are my only chance. Rania."

The shot missed the deer's heart, striking above the back thigh, shattering bone. The bullet's impact knocked the animal on its side, but it got quickly back to its feet and clomped into the thicket. The blood shone blue on its back.

"Go after it," they called from the neighboring tower. The ladder creaked loudly as he climbed down. He opened the chamber and reloaded the gun. He began to follow the trail of blood, dead leaves crackling under his feet. He followed the trail for a few minutes before he heard the animal's whimpering. A wounded deer cries like a child. It wasn't hard to zero in on the source of the noise.

The deer lay on its side. It kicked the air with its forelegs; it could no longer stand. The area was filled with the sound of its crying, its nostrils quivering and steamy, its eyes open wide. The young man held the rifle to his shoulder and was preparing to shoot when he remembered how much his father hated it when he wasted bullets. He took out his knife and used it to cut the artery on the deer's neck. The crying was soon overtaken by a deep gasping, and in under ten seconds the deer expired. He wiped the knife clean with a handful of dry leaves.

Footsteps approached, and his father emerged from the thicket.

"That was beautiful, for not having shot in a year."

"I didn't hit it right."

"It won't be left out in the forest, that's the main thing. Tomorrow we won't have to go sniffing around for the rotting carcass. We can call it a day."

The young man put the deer on his shoulder and they began back to the cabin. The clouds covered the moon. The forest was bathed in darkness, but they knew the path. The cabin was modest and simply furnished, with a wood stove, three beds, a big rough table, and chairs with comfortable cushions. The hunters drank cold beer as they skillfully cleaned the deer. There was one month left in summer.

The Field

The mine had torn his left ankle apart. Because of the flies he took off his shirt and spread it over the stump, then wound his belt tightly around his leg where the artery was. He watched the bugs feast on the blood from the soaked-through material.

In Chad, in the area between Abéché and Gaga, there were hardly any villages. The road was impassable due to the season's rain. The river, which dried up during the summer months, surged over almost everything, due to the two months of continual showers. When the rainy season finally ended, the riverbeds were full with drinking water and the country was covered in green. Flowers grew red by the riverside, and the desert was kinder to its inhabitants. The entire phenomenon, however, wouldn't last longer than a month.

Adam Abdelkarim lay squinting in the knee-high grass. It was approaching noon. He was perhaps thirty miles from Abéché. If he strained to see, he could make out the Sudanese border. His phone buzzed with each passing minute, the device signaling that it was running out of power. Nor did he have enough credit to make a call. He looked down at his leg and caught the smell of his own blood and flesh.

He had left the backpack that was stuffed full of children's books behind him. He hadn't tried to drag it with him to the road, because every movement brought unbelievable pain. He had already come close to fainting when he tied off the bleeding artery.

It's true. I shouldn't have come, he thought. *But I am so close*. He closed his eyes.

When the white foreigners had been evacuated, they'd all gathered together in the canteen. A drunk Belgian was shouting at the top of his lungs that this was the "last supper," but otherwise it was mostly quiet. People just ate and tried to use their phones. There hadn't been a signal since early morning; the rebels had seen to that. The canteen's black workers nervously circulated with water pitchers. There was speculation about what would happen next, but exactly what that was, nobody could say for sure.

In Chad there were eight different armies in constant battle. The two most prominent were the national army and the United Front for Democratic Change; the former was in government hands, the latter recruited from the smaller tribes along the Sudanese borderlands.

Fighting would break out at the end of each rainy season, with the rebels desperately trying to take the capital, N'Djamena. Nobody knew exactly why they were fighting; they had simply grown accustomed to the continual war that two generations had been raised with. Over time slogans like "Change," "Democracy," and "Unity" wore away in direct proportion with the amount of Chinese or Russian ammunition fired. Only the tribal affiliations and the appetite for wealth remained for those who took part in the fighting. Few could resist. Everything was worth dying for: manliness, honor, a woman, arable land, enemy tribes' property;

or perhaps they just fought to do away with the creeping rot of boredom that came with the rainy season.

During the rainy season, however, there was no war, because the roads were impassible. The government and the rebels forged a fragile peace agreement, which grew stronger with the first storm's raindrops. Everyone was of one mind in this respect: while the showers fell, the fighting ceased. But there hadn't been a drop in a week. Military action was flaring up in the east of the country.

Adam thought of Susan, the Englishwoman, and her scent of lavender. He pictured her light blue scarf. Under his foot he felt the gravel of the humanitarian base. Adam tried to recall their last conversation. The woman was around twenty years older. The base wasn't ready yet, and she had been the first white person to arrive.

They were sitting at one of the canteen's plastic tables, the wind catching the woman's hat.

"You speak English beautifully," she said. Adam thanked her. He'd learned English from a Sudanese Christian missionary. His father had wanted that for him.

"Do you know what it means to be a humanitarian?" asked the woman.

"To teach English to refugee children."

"No. To be a humanitarian you need only do things for other people."

The wind blew the woman's hat from her head. Adam didn't remember how the conversation ended, but it didn't matter. *I always note the important things*, he thought. He remembered that Susan had a son who was addicted to cocaine back in London. Adam had never been to London, but he knew that an awful lot of people lived there. "Cocaine addiction is a sickness," Susan said. Along with it comes a lot of suffering. *Their suffering is ob-*

viously greater than mine. Everything is greater with white people, Adam thought and looked at his ankle. The shirt was already sutured to it with dried blood. Somebody was bound to come this way sooner or later. He stuck his head up from the grass and spied the road, but other than a few birds, he didn't see a thing. Adam was sure that someone from the nearest town would herd their animals here to drink, by nightfall at the latest. He could stay alive that long, no problem. It was just a matter of having enough water. He reached out a hand for his plastic bottle. The water was warm, and ran down his chin.

"To be a humanitarian you need only do things for other people," he had explained to Mireille in the village. They were sitting in their adobe hut. Mireille was seventeen when he paid a bride price of 200 dollars—enough to live on around there for two years—to her father. He wasn't sorry. For him that was just two months' pay, thanks to the whites. Mireille raised her eyebrows. She still didn't understand the word's meaning.

"Then in our village everybody is a humanitarian."

"No, you have to work with people outside of the tribe. The whites have no tribes," he tried to explain, before alighting on a better example. "Being a humanitarian means the same as being a good Muslim. Only that the whites don't know this."

The answer must have satisfied the girl, because she reached out and stroked his cheek. She offered him milk, but he didn't want any. He just watched how the warm goat milk flowed into her mouth. He loved her, but he couldn't say why. Perhaps because she was the first to offer him something to drink when he came across the border from Sudan. Perhaps it was because she had the lightest colored palms from among the village girls.

Adam heard a car engine and machine-gun fire. He sat up and saw that a United Front truck was coming up the road. Eight passengers were riding in the back, all off to the fighting. At least three from the group were not yet fifteen years old. He could tell which army they belonged to from the robes they wore. Adam gritted his teeth and kept down. He knew what it would mean if they noticed him; not one of them was of his tribe. He shuddered for a moment, thinking they had seen him, because the truck slowed, then stopped. The soldiers went to the largest pool of water and filled their canteens. He watched as the younger ones kicked around a stone as if they were playing soccer.

He had watched the championship game with the rest of the humanitarian workers. Everybody was rooting for Cameroon; they were playing Egypt, and they won. On the base there was no difference between the whites and the blacks, at least that's what Susan said. Only that the black canteen workers always served meals first to the whites, who gave them bigger tips than the local black employees.

He rarely went to the base. He had worked in Goz Beïda for five months. When the contract expired, he went to Abéché to pick up his pay. Lots of the Sudanese refugees lived in Goz Beïda. He taught their children the ABCs in English. By now they knew enough of the language to buy a hat.

In the refugee camps everybody loved the whites, because they knew they had them to thank for their flour. When SUVs arrived at night, children ran out alongside them, and women waved from the huts. The camps were bigger than any city in the country. And they had their own militias, so they could protect themselves from the smaller groups of raiding bandits. This, however, didn't deter the larger armies, which did what they knew best. A refugee camp was the best place if an army wanted to replenish its ranks or indulge its soldiers' sexual appetites. In a country where there are simply too many laws to possibly obey, a man with a rifle in his hand is God himself.

He knew the belt around his leg had come loose, because the shirt began to redden again. The soldiers had already departed and nobody was on the road. When he retied the belt, he felt dizzy. Slowly night was falling. Adam thought about how the cocaine users must suffer.

The first SUV had arrived at the base at ten. Confusion was already taking hold. The base's administration—Susan among them—had placed guards at the blue-painted entrance. By the door they set up a table to check passports. Everybody stood in a line. It was very hot and the men were sweating through their shirts.

"Those with European passports go first," said Susan as she packed. She had already placed the framed picture of her with the Sudanese children of the camp in her suitcase. Adam's expression must have been one of abject fright, because the woman stopped packing when she saw his face.

"Wouldn't it be possible for my wife and me to go?" he asked.

"Not now. First the Europeans need to go."

"But I am also a humanitarian."

"I know," the woman said as she resumed packing. "Don't be afraid; we'll be back soon. Nothing will happen here like in Darfur. We won't allow it."

"And when are you coming back?"

"Within a few days. A week at the most."

"Then I will go and tell my wife not to worry," Adam said with a smile.

"You shouldn't be on the road now. Wait until the fighting ends," said Susan, and with her suitcase in hand headed off toward the entrance.

It was a clear starry sky, more so than usual. A chilly wind blew. Adam was about an hour's walk from the village. He began to shiver. He felt the belt cut into his flesh. He had already lost a lot of blood. Adam looked down at his leg, and thought it was so white it couldn't have been his own. He peered into the darkness on the road, straining to see. No movement. *It's possible that the townsfolk only come to water their animals in the morning*, he thought. *I am strong. I can last until then. I was always strong.*

He thought about streetlights, how he would be able to see much better if only the road were lit with them. The topic had come up with Susan once. In London everything is lit up. In France too. At night all of Europe is flooded with light. Only Africa stays dark at night. Surely in Europe you'd be able to see the village lights.

The crackle of machine guns sounded along with grenade bursts. In the distance something began to glow. It lasted twenty minutes, then the weapons went quiet, and all he could hear were the bugs in the grass. *Probably the United Front was trading fire with the national army*, thought Adam. *The village wasn't the target; because of the whites they wouldn't dare. They must have lit a few houses from the outskirts on fire. The houses there burn easier.*

He remembered that once, when he was a child, he had nearly set their hut alight after he'd stolen his father's pipe to test it out. His father had lashed him with a belt for that. Adam had no idea where his father was now. Somewhere in Darfur, in a village, if there were still villages in Darfur. *This isn't Darfur*, he thought, and shook off his worries. He never understood why, on the TV they watched in the canteen, the tribes' names were never mentioned in news broadcasts. Otherwise, the information didn't mean anything to anybody.

Adam looked at his leg. It wasn't bleeding anymore. He determined that if he were to cut off the foot, he would be able to move. Perhaps he could drag himself to the village. He took out the knife and considered how to go about the job. To remove the foot he would have to cut the remaining tendons. The bone had been blown in two by the shrapnel, so he wouldn't need to contend with that. He had witnessed similar operations in Abéché, in the hospital. There were children who, while herding animals, had stepped on a mine or an unexploded grenade. The goal in every case was to keep the limb from turning gangrenous and stemming the spread of infection. These days, lots of kids in the village market square played soccer with one leg and a crutch.

It spooked him that the cutting didn't hurt at all. But it was over fast. He tried to crawl to the road, but he was weaker than he'd thought. After a few yards he gave up and passed out.

He saw his wife before him, how they made love. Recalling how good her scent was, he saw flowers in front of him and felt the touch of her skin.

Adam slowly came to. People were moving on the road. Civilians. Men, women, and children were running into the field. He held out his hand. A man found him. The man leaned into the grass and whispered that the United Front had declared the villagers enemies and began to shoot everybody. They had shot at least ten people in the head in the village square and had rounded up the women. Those who were still alive were fleeing. Adam stayed quiet. He asked the man if he knew where the soldiers were heading. "West," said the man, who ran onward. In the field, mines exploded, and the sound of moaning filled the morning air. Adam couldn't see the other wounded, but he heard their voices.

Don't worry, he thought. *This couldn't happen in my village. The whites are coming back; they wouldn't abandon us.* For a while he listened to the whimpering from the field. The soldiers then arrived there from the direction of the village, and one after another shot the wounded in the head. After a while everything became silent and only the sound of insects could be heard. The warm smell of blood drifted across the field.

In the waiting room of Heathrow International, Susan sipped her coffee and looked impatiently at her watch. Her husband had called to say he would be a few minutes late. Sitting across from her was a young man who had studied political science at Cambridge. They had sat next to each other on the plane after he boarded in Libya. They talked about Chad, how the United Front had reached the capital, N'Djamena. The man was interested in what the United Nations would do.

"You know, the humanitarians will do as much as they can for them," said Susan, and took another sip of coffee. She grimaced. It had already gone cold.

"But everybody has already been evacuated from there," said the man.

"Yes, none of our people remain. Unfortunately, it's like this when the army comes. We have to go, and there is simply nothing to be done about it. But we always return."

"When will you go back?" asked the man.

"It depends on the political situation. Maybe in three months, maybe a year. But don't worry about Chad; there's no ethnic cleansing there. It's not Darfur."

Meanwhile Susan's husband had arrived. She finished her coffee and changed to her local SIM card. She was late: the city's street lights were already blazing.

The Desert Is Cold In the Morning

Hail nothing full of nothing,
nothing is with thee.

—Ernest Hemingway

Father really was dead. I was at an editorial meeting when the doctor told me the news. Twice I said I couldn't take his call before he was able to inform me. He said, "Your father is dead," and I said, "So what." He told me that he wasn't able to contact my brother in Berlin, so I'd have to return home and take care of the papers. And there was the dog. The doctor was a friend of the family. He'd already seen to the cremation.

I knew the old man was ill, and I had been expecting his death, though I never thought he would kick the bucket on such a chilly Wednesday, after lunch. He was well known for his sense of timing: he had missed my high school graduation banquet due to a drawn-out hunters' party.

So, like I said, I was standing there in the editorial office, listening to the evaluation of the latest issue of the magazine by our know-it-all editor-guy, and I seriously resented the fact that I had to leave town. When the meeting was over I followed the editors to the cafeteria. By 3 PM there was nothing left but cheap, 650-forint plates of batter-fried cheese with tartar sauce. So I chose the fried cheese. The taste of a dead father is that of fried cheese soaked in oil with overcooked rice, vinegary tartar sauce, and a few slices of cucumber. I left my plate shining and empty.

My photographer drove me over the Danube to the Pest side of Budapest. I went into a café to drink a coffee. I opened my laptop to check the schedule for trains to the provinces. I bought some drugs to make what was to come more bearable. "I always calm down on amphetamines," I said to myself as I purchased five grams. It was still a bit sticky when I slid the paper-wrap into a little pocket on the side of my moleskin pants. By seven that night I was at Keleti railway station, ticket in hand. Adult fare, round-trip. The ticket cost 8,000 forints.

I sat in the buffet car on the westbound train that left Budapest. The journey to Csorna took four coffees, three beers, half a pack of cigarettes, and a somewhat decent fuck in the bathroom with the forty-something blonde from behind the counter. The tracks running farther west, to Szombathely and Sopron near the Austrian border, parted at Csorna. The buffet car with the blonde headed for Szombathely.

I drank four more coffees—instant—and got permission to smoke as long as the window was open. I knew where we were with my eyes closed. For an entire semester at university I'd traveled slumped next to this window.

I arrived at the station at 10:35, my shirt reeking of sweat and of the particular odor of the Hungarian State Railways. The station looked the same as it had for the last ten years, with the same old welcoming slogans posted for arriving passengers to see: "Welcome to the town of fidelity and freedom," and "Don't forget: the cyclamen is an endangered flower!" I recognized a few of the gypsies hanging out in front of the station's bar—we had gone to school together.

I got off the train, with only my laptop dangling from my shoulder. I walked past families embracing; first-year students met by their parents in the vestibule. I'd been met by my parents like this some time ago. Not anymore.

I took a cab home. Neighbors peeked out to see who was coming. There was a "For Sale" sign in the window. Our house was the most repulsive imitation farmhouse on the street. It was painted a pale shade of light green. A dead geranium was rotting on the windowsill. I never could understand why the pale green, why my mother chose this very color. The cellar window was open. Somewhere in the gloom behind that window I'd lost my virginity. It wasn't pretty.

I paid for the cab and fished for the keys in my pocket. Father's dog barked behind the door. It took me three tries to find the right key. The dog was sitting by the bottom step of the foyer staircase, sweeping the floor with his tail. When he saw me enter, he threw himself on his back, belly to the sky. He was expecting me to scratch him; he was whining with joy because he recognized my smell. Bootsi, the wire-haired dachshund. Ten years old and thirty pounds.

I opened all the windows and cleaned the dog shit from the carpet. The ambulance driver had closed the front door, so Bootsi couldn't get out to take care of his business. I poured water into a bowl and he drank. I looked around for something that could pass for dry dog food, filled his bowl, then entered my father's room. The dog refused to leave me alone for a minute.

I had carried Bootsi home myself from a nearby village some ten years ago. He was small enough to fit in my palm. I hadn't thought he would survive the first winter. He was the scraggliest of the litter, which is why my mother chose him. Up until her dying day, she was convinced that in the end it was always the youngest son who turned out to be the smartest, the luckiest, and the happiest, like in fairy tales. So that must have been the reason behind her choice. My brother and I had been begging for a dog for seventeen years. Finally my parents got themselves one.

I don't know how he did it, but Bootsi the dachshund turned my parents into avid dog lovers in a under a year. He was small and constantly crying, but would calm down when my mother picked him up. It got to the point where the three of them slept side by side in the conjugal bed: mom, dad, and the dog. They were convinced that the animal understood everything. After my brother and I moved to Pest, they began confusing our names with Bootsi's. He became their last child.

I reclined into my father's armchair, in front of his desk. His computer was still on. I cancelled his downloads and I checked my email. My brother was desperately sorry he could not come.

The dog was lying at my feet, looking up at me from time to time. Noticing I had taken off my boots and socks, he began to lick my toes. I shouted at him, and he ran to hide under the table. I looked around for a place to sleep. My father's bed still held his imprint. I spent some time looking for sheets and blankets, with the dog close at my heels. After rummaging through the apartment, I came up with no sheets but a half a bottle of Metaxa. I slumped into my father's chair again, methodically sipping from the bottle as I deleted his stuff from the computer. The dachshund sat back on his hindquarters and placed his paws on my knee. He would have already jumped up on my lap by now, but he was aging and having problems with his spine. He was waiting for me to lift him. He'd wait in vain. I brushed off his paws and told him to leave me alone. Bootsi crawled back under the bed. I finished the bottle and collapsed into Father's bed, fully dressed.

I opened my eyes to find Bootsi's muzzle facing me on the pillow. He was sleeping with his tongue hanging out of his mouth. I had no idea how he'd managed to get up the on bed, but somehow he'd managed. I felt his breath on my face. But I had a headache and no energy to get pissed off. I climbed out of bed and lit a cigarette. It was nine o'clock. I was already late. The notary public was waiting for me, but before that I had to get my father's papers together and pay for the cremation. The dog raised his head and looked at me. He walked me to the door; I had to push him back to get rid of him.

I got home at four. I was sweating; I hadn't eaten anything all day. I visited the supermarket next door and bought some cold cuts, rolls, and milk. I asked if they had any cardboard boxes. I chose some and hauled them home over a few trips. The dog was waiting for me by the door with his legs in the air. I stroked his belly, and then went into my father's study. I started to eat. Bootsi followed my every bite with his sad eyes. I lost my appetite and gave him all of the cold cuts. This calmed him; he lay down next to my legs, and soon began to snore.

I looked over his silvery coat as he slept. He was evidently thinking I was there to live with him from then on. That I was the new boss. He was wrong. Budapest is not the place for a ten-year-old dachshund and dog walking was not my forte. He wouldn't even be able to climb the stairs in my building.

I went to take a shower. Bootsi sat in front of the shower stall, waiting patiently. I dried myself with a towel, rubbed my hair dry, and chose a shirt from my father's wardrobe. Then I decided to reward myself. I measured out two lines and snorted. I used a page from my father's notebook to roll a straw for the purpose. I packed dishes, clothes, and books until two in the morning. My progress was good; I almost finished the job, except for my father's room.

I took Hemingway's *The Winner Takes Nothing* from the bookshelf and read it all the way through. The drug did not let me sleep until four. By that time, I had listened to all my father's jazz standards from his computer, and I watched some YouTube videos to take the edge off the jazz. Before going to sleep I made sure to put the dog out of the room and close the door. He whined from the other side for a while before going silent.

I woke at ten staring into the dog's face. The door was open; he must have waited until I fell asleep then jumped at it. The weight of his body had opened the door. He lay unabashedly close to me, our heads level. I climbed out of bed, lit a cigarette, and put on one of my father's shirts. I noticed a photograph on the wall showing my mother holding the dachshund in her hands when he was still quite small. *No more of that*, I thought. Mother had died years ago.

I stepped out into the hall and saw that Bootsi had taken revenge by shitting on the carpet. And there he was, at my heels again. I wanted to kick him, but he lay on his back and threw his legs up. I stroked his belly, cleaned up after him, and scanned the household for the leash. I found it above the gas meter. The lead was plastic, its length adjustable with a button.

Bootsi walked down the street with great determination. The vet's office was not very far, and when he realized where we were heading, he slowed down. He did not like the vet, though he had been a regular visitor there for ten years, with all kind of ailments. The money my mother left with Dr. Kovach could have bought ten litters of dachshunds. But the doctor liked the dog. Bootsi was a regular customer.

I opened up the green gate, letting us into the front yard. Then we opened the front door and entered the waiting room. The dog, shaking from head to toe, hid between my legs. I stared at the hospital-green tiles and the advertisements for pet food. I read everything you could want to know about ticks, parasites, and canine health in the pamphlets left out for visitors.

The door opened and the doctor appeared in a white apron. He was approaching sixty and was somewhat flabby. I had to drag the skittish dog into his office. The shelves there held an array of medicine. A great white table stood in the middle of the room—that was where the doctor operated on the pets of the neighborhood. I grabbed the dog and placed him on the table. He kept his tail down, but licked my hand as I held him.

The doctor expressed his condolences for my father. I thanked him. He asked why I had come and I told him: I wanted the dog put to sleep. He said no. Bootsi was a good dog; he had good genes, and couldn't be killed just like that. He told me to consider how important he'd been to my parents. I insisted that going to sleep peacefully would be the most humane solution for the dog, but it was all in vain; he didn't want to hear of it. "I just can't do it," he said. He gave Bootsi a dog biscuit and walked us to the exit. The dog collapsed on the ground and refused to move. I had no choice; I picked him up and carried the animal home in my arms.

Arriving at the house, I gave him some food and went to my father's room to enjoy the ten solitary minutes it would take Bootsi to eat. Then he returned to his place at my feet. I went to the kitchen to get a glass of water. I looked at his bowl. He had left half of his food uneaten. As if that were my portion.

The next day I awoke to find the dog in bed with me again. I dressed, and went to the bank to withdraw some money. I paid the required fee to register the property ownership transfer. Now the house legally belonged to my brother and me. I sat in a pub, drank beer, and ate fried sausages, swabbing up the grease with a slice of bread. I bought two newspapers, read them, and left them in the pub for the next customer.

On the way home, I was overcome by disgust for the town. I felt nauseous as I walked by the places I knew from my childhood and I wished I could get back to Budapest as soon as possible. Or anywhere else. Just out of here. Away from this place.

With my father gone, I had no more ties to this town. I looked at the streets and I felt like I was looking at the husk of a huge dead insect. I couldn't find a single nostalgic thought in myself. I had boxed away everything that could be salvaged.

The real estate agency called in the afternoon to inform me they had an inquiry on the house. I went home and was greeted by the dog. He was whimpering with joy upon my return.

I started to pack, again with the dog at my heels. It occurred to me that it would be better not to let the new owners see that an animal was also living there.

I rang the neighbor's doorbell. Terike opened the door. She lamented at length about how bad it must be for me, dead father and all. She sobbed a bit and asked if she could help in any way. I asked to borrow her tiny Suzuki sedan for an hour. I said I had to take care of some administrative stuff. She looked awfully sorry for the ignition key when she handed it to me, saying, "Take care of it."

I attached the leash to the dog again. He excitedly plodded after me. Father used to take him for long walks. He probably missed those walks. I sat him on the passenger seat, where he went quiet. They used to drive in Terike's car a lot. I knew exactly where to go. There was a clearing far enough out of town. I used to pick mushrooms there when I was a kid.

We drove for twenty minutes, the dog staring out the window the whole time. The sky was the color of milk, the wind was picking up, and it was getting cold out. We drove up the winding forest road, and then, when the clearing came into view, I cut the engine. I opened the door for the dog; he jumped out and sprinted away on the grass. "Great!" I said. "Live happily and hunt for rabbits!" I turned on the ignition and drove away. The dog ran after the car for a bit before giving up. I drove home, showed some prospective buyers around the house, and then threw myself into bed.

In the morning I ironed a shirt from my father's wardrobe. I shaved and dressed. I had to visit the real estate agency to agree on the price and sign the contract. I drank coffee, opened a jar of cherry preserves, and had breakfast. I tried on all my father's jackets but none fit, so I left the house in my own leather jacket. A thirty-something brunette greeted me in the agency. She told me to pay the gas and electricity bills, and bring her copies of the receipts so we could sign a contract the next day. Arranging all this took up the larger part of the day.

I didn't get back to my parents' house until late evening. The dachshund was waiting for me by the front door. His hair was matted and filthy, but there he was, his tail wagging. He had found his way home over hedges and across ditches. I must have left the front gate open, allowing him into the yard. He licked my hand and jumped up on my legs. I pushed him off and went to the computer to check my email. He dashed after me and sat close to my feet.

I had two emails. The first had come from my girlfriend saying she could no longer share her life with me. The other had come from a literary editor as a reply to one of the short stories I had submitted. He rejected it, writing, "The desert is cold in the morning, and since you suggest that it is not, this casts doubt on the authenticity of the story." I was in no mood to disagree.

I decided to take it easy for the rest of the day. I sniffed half a gram of amphetamines from off the cover of my father's favorite volume of poetry, and then went over to the shop to get a bottle of booze. In small-town supermarkets, expensive drinks are kept on the top shelf behind the counter. The shop clerk used to be my classmate. She was part of the disco crowd, had a dolphin tattoo, and would not even go to the toilet without putting on a ton of make-up. She recognized me. She said she was sorry about my father and wanted to leave the provinces as well.

She scribbled her phone number on the back of the receipt she handed me, and said, "Call me!" I bought bourbon and seltzer.

I returned to the house. The dog was waiting at the door. I went to my father's room and opened the bourbon to let it breathe. I poured water into a glass and waited. The dog jumped up on the bed and went to sleep. I was thinking about an appropriate response to the editor, but none came to mind. The amphetamines were really kicking in, so I set myself to packing up my parents' belongings and picking out what I could use in Budapest.

I began to take books off the shelf. Christian philosophers: Maritain, Chardin, Weil—my father's favorites—and next to them: Marx. My father had a Social Democrat's view of Catholicism. Why not take these back to the city? Next to them was a family photo album. I swept it off the shelf and onto the floor. I didn't need that shit. The pictures scattered in every direction. I poured a glass of bourbon, added seltzer, and drank.

Sometime later that night, I almost stepped on one of the photographs. It was from 1992 and showed my brother and me in fatigues, saluting into the camera. He was nine, I was twelve. I remembered that summer. We'd taken a vacation to Zalakaros, a country town down south best known as a bathing resort. One day I failed to buy the tickets to the public bath and I also lost track of my brother. My father said I was a good-for-nothing and not much would come of me. I had bought a toy gun with the money I'd saved on the tickets. He smacked me and told me to stay clear of him for a while, that I was irresponsible and spent his hard-earned money on all kinds of shit.

The old man came down with a fever that night. My mother took care of him. When I went in to see him, he told me to get out of the room. He added that if by any chance he died, I shouldn't come to the funeral. They don't need people like me there. Of course, later on there was a great reconciliation: he told me he loved me and so on. Mother said I was the more important son.

I collected the fallen photographs and put them back on the shelf. I sniffed an additional 0.4 grams of amphetamines—from the top of the photograph this time. I drank one more glass of bourbon. I watched the dog sleeping in the bed. I must have spent a long time observing him, because suddenly he looked up at me. It occurred to me that time had proven my father right: I was a slacker and I couldn't accomplish a thing. I couldn't even get rid of this damned dog.

I called for Bootsi. He grunted as he hopped off the bed: his leg hurt. Every dachshund has problems with its spine by the time it gets old. Still, Bootsi came quickly, as quick as an old dachshund could, wagging his tail.

"Let's go play ball," I said to him. I took a swig from the bottle, then tucked it under my arm and started for the yard. The dog came after me in something like delight. It was 3 AM.

I took the back stairs; he followed my steps cautiously. I turned on the outdoor lighting. The shabby yard lit up in front of me. The shed next to where we used to grill meat in the summer was overgrown with wild grape vines and knee-high weeds. The dog put a ball down in front of me. I kicked it for him. He ran after it.

I began to get cold, and thought I should go back to the house to get a jacket. But first I wanted to take care of this business. Fueled by the drug, I felt my heart banging inside my chest. I looked around and by the wall I found the axe Father used to prune bushes with. I picked it up and saw its head had begun to rust. The weight of it sobered me up a bit.

Bootsi was slow to bring the ball back because he got distracted by smells and trailed off. I was in no hurry. He finally came back, dropping the ball in front of my feet, looking up excitedly, wagging his tail. I didn't give him time to realize what was happening. I aimed for the best spot and struck; he let out a moan and dropped dead. *That's it for the dog,* I thought. *I'll bury him in the morning.*

I took a long pull on the bourbon and went back to the house. I dropped the axe, went upstairs, and collapsed on the bed without undressing. My father was right: I was irresponsible.

My dreams were filled with all sorts of absurdities, including being lost in the desert with people I couldn't talk to. My tongue was swollen from the bourbon and was stuck dry to the top of my mouth like a piece of gauze. I opened my eyes.

Bootsi was there next to me. The gore from his wound was spread across the bed sheet. He woke up to me waking up, and began wagging his tail. His hair was caked into the wound on his head. I examined it; it wasn't very deep. I sat up and the ball fell into my hand.

I went to the bathroom. I looked into the mirror; my face was streaked with blood. Bootsi had followed in my steps, a bit slower than usual. I found no trace of injury on myself; he must have licked my face in my sleep: the blood was his. I took a shower. I stepped out of the stall; the aftereffects of the previous night bore down on me and I staggered forward. My stomach felt like it was the size of the head of a pin.

I walked to the café for a coffee. I smoked two cigarettes and came to the decision that at all costs I would return to Budapest that very day. It was ten in the morning and freezing outside. I called the vet again; I had to let it ring a long time before he picked up. He asked how the dog was. I told him he was okay. I had enough of small talk, and told him I would sue him if he refused to put him to sleep. I would cause him to lose his veterinary license, and punish him for fucking around with the owner of the dog. Instead of an answer I listened to a long silence, before he finally agreed to see us at five. I hung up.

I dropped by the real estate agency and signed the papers. I would only have to wait for my brother to send the copies back from Berlin with his signature and then we would get our money. But I didn't need to stay in town to wait for that. I asked Terike to box up the remaining books and stuff, telling her that if she needed any of the furniture, she should take it. I didn't want any of it. I told the agent I was leaving the house with the furniture in it. I would return in a week to take some of the boxes.

At home, the dog was on my heels wherever I went. He pushed his bloodied head into my hands to be petted. I realized I couldn't take him to the vet like that, so I put him into the tub and poured warm water all over him. I cleaned his wound carefully and washed him with dog shampoo. He endured it without a sound; he only licked my hand a few times and lapped up the water from the tub.

I dried him with the same towel I had used on myself in the morning. He shook his body and begged himself up onto my lap. I lifted him. He licked my face.

I put his leash on him at quarter to five. He became suddenly excited, assuming we were going for another walk. We headed out alright, but I had drag him, trembling, to the vet. In the waiting room he hid between my legs and got me tangled in the leash. I took it off his neck and put it in my pocket. An old lady came out of the vet's office with her cat. It was our turn.

I had to lift up Bootsi and carry him into the examination room. He was trembling all over but I held him tight, which calmed him. He licked my face. I placed him on the middle of the operating table, where he tried to stand straight as he shook. I had to stroke him to keep him calm. The doctor drew some kind of tranquilizer into his syringe and told me to hold the dog down. There was no real need for it, though, because Bootsi had no intention of fleeing. I held him tight anyway. The doctor injected the tranquilizer; we waited a little, and I rubbed his neck until he lay down. Then came the next shot, the lethal dose. The dog lay motionless: he did nothing to stop us, he let us do our job.

The doctor handed me a dog biscuit and told me to give it to him, so he could experience something nice while passing away. I tried to give it to him, but he did not care to take it. He licked my hand instead. I missed the moment he stopped breathing.

I paid 6,000 forints for the injections and an additional 4,000 for the disposal of the body. I left the vet's office and reached into my pocket for my cigarettes. There I found his leash. I pulled it out and looked it over. There was a sticker with Bootsi's name on it, along with a request for anyone who happened to find the lost dog to call my father, in return for a reward.

I left the clinic, tossed the leash into the first trash bin I found, and lit a cigarette. Snowflakes began to descend, slow and heavy. I walked down to the station. I was freezing. I just wanted to catch the night train, drink some cognac, and drop in on my local pub. The next day I'd buy a plane ticket to the Middle East. I'd leave and never return. The snowflakes melted on the warmth of my scalp, collected into tiny streams, and poured down my face.

The Majestic Clouds

Around noon the black clouds appear seemingly from nowhere. Majestic clouds, thick and dark. They hang in the center of the sky like mirages. They appear contemplative, reaching toward the horizon, their color not much different from tar. Unbelievably majestic clouds suspended in the sky, dirty and black, darkening at the center. Clouds unlike those seen in the skies of Europe. Their sudden appearance signals that the rainy season has come to the Sudanese frontier.

Marosh doesn't show the slightest interest in the clouds. He sits in the communications tent and nervously taps away at his laptop. The tent for the foreigners was erected at the camp's periphery, on the hilltop. The NGO keeps its satellite phone and technical equipment there, which is how it got its name. It's the only reliable Internet connection within two hundred miles, a weak signal from a twenty-foot-high antennae rising through the tarp.

If you stand by the entrance, you can see the entire refugee camp spreading out in front of you all the way to the red hills beyond.

Not many people live in the foreigners' camp. The medical personnel are twenty in total. They are mostly Canadian volunteers, veterans who have already assisted in multiple humanitarian catastrophes across Africa. Marosh, at age twenty-six, is the youngest there. That he works as a journalist further sets him apart from the others. He types feverishly, bent over his laptop. Sweat paints stains on his shirt and drips down under his arms.

"At nine this morning they carried out the rite of passage," he writes. "The foundation's ranking doctor met at length with the Zaghawa elders, but he couldn't talk them out of the genital circumcision of a group of twelve-year-old girls, an operation performed by women of the tribe. Initially the tribal leaders approved the doctors' assistance in case of complications during the procedure, then the *marabou*, the refugee camp's religious leader, declared the foreigners' presence immoral and ordered them from the tent."

After he finishes the paragraph, he rises from his camping chair. He reaches into his pants pocket and fishes out a cigarette. The lighter is slippery in the sweat of his hand; it takes a few tries to light the cigarette. Marosh takes a drag, sits, then rests his head in his hands and stares at the monitor.

They won't print it, he thinks, and pictures his editor's face twenty-five hundred miles away. Marosh had been given explicit instructions to avoid stories like this. He wasn't supposed to write human-interest stories. The articles were strictly to be about tribal movement, the humanitarian conditions in the camps, and things pertaining to the heightening conflict in the Darfur crisis.

Female circumcision had nothing to do with the mission. They had been doing these procedures for a thousand years in this land. Seeing the preparations, the doctors objected, of course, but couldn't dissuade the tribesmen, who said the labia and clitoris were not pleasing to the eye, plus the ritual was thought to set the girls on the proper moral path. Moreover, they insisted that if the ritual wasn't carried out, the girls would be unable to find husbands. They simply wouldn't be considered normal.

Marosh had photographed the entire preparation, up to the moment when the older women opened a box of blue packaged scalpel blades and led the young girls to the curtained-off room. He became unsettled only on recognizing Mara among the group. He had traveled with her and her family from Daru to the refugee camp. They'd traveled in a covered United Nations truck, the trip up the red dirt road lasting three hours in the day's broiling heat. The Janjaweed, the militia of the government in Khartoum, had demolished their village in an act of ethnic cleansing. The bodies of the dead were left unburied; Mara's family were the only ones left alive. Marosh didn't ask how they survived the attack, didn't ask what they had been through; he only stared at the child's dirty face and blank expression.

Marosh broke the ice by pulling a half-melted bar of chocolate from his pocket. Swiss chocolate, he had bought it in Libya at the duty-free shop, on the way to Chad. He had even forgotten he had it, but the girl's expression brought it to mind, as it was a basic fact of life that sweets cheered kids up.

"Chocolate," he said, and held out the bar. The girl looked at it blankly, so he repeated, "Chocolate."

The child, in a skittish motion, took the bar, bit off a piece, then smiled when she discovered its taste.

"Mara," she said, indicating herself, as she chewed.

"Daniel," said Marosh, and took her picture.

Nothing more had happened. Since their arrival a few days passed during which the girl was sure to smile and wave at Marosh if she saw him at the refugee camp market. Marosh wasn't surprised when he discovered the girl was among those to be circumcised, but became alarmed when the chief banished the doctors from the tent.

From the group of six girls, Mara was the only one who developed complications. What they were he didn't know yet, just that she didn't emerge from the tent on her own two feet like the rest.

Marosh had a hazy idea about the operation, which he gathered from what he read on the Internet, though he wasn't familiar with the exact local practice. A few hours after the procedure was supposed to be completed, he heard voices coming from the tent. At first he thought that it was the sound of animals or a cat's yowling. But there weren't any cats in the camp. It was then that Marosh fled the refugee area and escaped back to the doctors' quarters.

Marosh leans back on a camping chair and takes a drag on his cigarette. The smoke scratches his throat. He looks at his watch: it's approaching five. *I'm not writing anything today*, he thinks. He steps out of the tent and is momentarily blinded by the clouds passing across the face of the sun, which is not shining at full strength anymore; you could look into it. The clouds are oily looking, appearing like a black bunch of grapes in the light. Marosh gazes at the sun as it reaches the hills beyond, the rocks' red outlines quivering when it disappears between them.

A few minutes pass before he realizes that music is playing. Quiet, solemn music, trickling scratchily between the tents. *Classical music*, he surmises, once he is able to make out the wind instruments and the singers' voices. *Somebody is listening to classical music.*

He heads toward the sound. He walks between the awnings of the tents, which stand facing each other, lined up along the length of the hill's periphery, to where the tent of Henderson, the head doctor, stands.

There, in front of the tent, sits Henderson, drinking whiskey, music coming from his laptop. Henderson is in his late fifties:

a severely balding man from Dublin, who has spent his whole life in Africa. You couldn't call him old though: the young volunteer doctors couldn't compete with his experience, though it's true, there wasn't a rush to try. Marosh is in the camp only through his permission.

"Good evening," says the man when he sees the journalist.

"Evening."

"Shall we share a drink?" he asks and holds the bottle out toward Marosh. Marosh drinks.

"Have a seat. Bring out a chair," says Henderson, and gestures toward the tent, where another camp chair sits by the bed. Marosh brings it out and sits.

"The afternoon was a stormy one."

"Yeah. I knew one of the children."

"I see."

"What will become of her?"

"We can't say right now. What's sure is that she lost lots of blood. She has a fever. Hopefully the wounds won't become completely infected, in which case there aren't many options. But, like I said, it's impossible to say what will happen."

"Shouldn't you help?"

"We can't do anything."

"It's cruelty."

"You are still quite young, which is why you don't understand. We can't risk an open conflict with the tribal leaders. If we don't keep to the rules, they won't cooperate with us. Then the mission will be a total failure. Imagine how many dead there would be if they didn't let us tend to the wounded. I feel bad for these children, but we can't risk it. In Africa, you need to make sacrifices."

"Okay," Marosh says. He feels a cramp in his stomach, and he shuts his eyes. In front of him he can picture the girl's small, undeveloped body, damp with sweat, black flies gathering around the blood.

"Have some more to drink. Relax. Tomorrow will bring a new day, with new problems. But today is over," says Henderson. He passes the bottle to the journalist; Marosh takes a long swig. When the whisky reaches his stomach, the cramping ceases. The alcohol takes effect. They sit for a few minutes listening to the music and looking up at the black clouds.

"Do you like opera?" asks Henderson.

"I don't really know much about it."

"Do you know what we are listening to right now?"

From the speaker comes the sound of two female singers performing a duet.

"No, but the tune is familiar."

"Really? From where?"

"It's the British Airways jingle. On TV these days."

Henderson smiles and takes a long swig, then continues.

"It's originally the 'Flower Duet' from *Lakmé*."

"The 'Flower Duet'?"

"Yes. The heroine and her servant are singing about flowers."

"Why?"

"Because they are young and the buds are opening. It takes place in India. Lakmé, the heroine, is the daughter of a high priest. She meets and falls in love with an English soldier. The conflict comes from their having different religions. Love, of course, overcomes this. The Hindus, however, stab Lakmé's love. Lakmé saves his life and nurses him back to health, and in the course of events she gives him her virtue."

"Beautiful," says Marosh.

"Isn't it? Now we would hope that story has a happy ending, but a friend of the man, named Frederic, appears and reminds him that it's his duty to join the war with his departing regiment, and he should leave the girl. And so he does, abandoning Lakmé."

Suddenly the sky rumbles. The clouds thunder so loudly that they drown out the music and Henderson's words can hardly be heard. The electric tension in the sky paints the air blue. A chill takes hold.

"The rain will start soon. But don't worry, the camp may get soaked, but we won't," says Henderson.

Marosh stares silently into the distance, then tosses the empty bottle. It makes a dull thud as it lands and rolls down the hillside. His mouth is totally dry, like that of a beginning drinker. He feels suddenly faint, though it comes with no real dizziness.

"If you like the music, I'll copy it for you," says Henderson.

"What will happen to the girl?" asks Marosh. "What will happen to the girl in the end?"

"Like in any good opera, she'll die."

"She'll die," Marosh says, though Henderson doesn't hear him from the mounting thunder. Thick, big drops of rain begin to fall, pelting the two of them wildly, with tropical rage. The two men stand a bit longer in front of the tent, staring at the storm. From the majestic clouds majestic lightning strikes at the camp.

The Strongest Knot

They let me know afterward that I'd died.

I had already been awake for an hour when the doctor arrived. He was short, the heavily bearded type; he said I had collapsed in the hotel lobby, and I was lucky that the ambulance arrived in time, because they were able to revive me on the way.

"It was an accident," I told the doctor, who seemed to take me at my word. In the Middle East the suicide rate is low, so much so that the news of one is reported in the papers, and word is passed quietly between men in the cafés.

I hadn't lied to the doctor; it really had been an accident. I simply wasn't able to sleep.

A person can bear the first forty-eight hours without sleep. It's after the seventy-second hour that the trouble starts. For example, you begin to see things that aren't there. By the 120th hour you simply can't distinguish reality from the nightmares spilling from your head. The nervous system smolders and pulses, like molten steel.

This is purely a physical condition, and has nothing to do with the soul. In this state, death is a pleasant option, compared to what's happening. There is nothing uplifting about going into shock.

Alcohol doesn't help, either. The nervous system may be in a stupor, but it continues to work without pause. After which there are the demons of dehydration and hangover to contend with. In stifling, forty-degree heat, in a seedy and roach-filled hotel room, it's nobody's idea of fun.

I decided to ask for medical attention after I'd rushed across a busy four-lane road, screaming that I needed to stop my wife, my child in her arms, from stepping into the street. A car's fender ripped the leg of my jeans and I almost broke my ankle before I made it to the other side. Of course my wife and child weren't even there.

After I wrapped my swollen ankle with my scarf, I got myself together and called Dr. Asim. I had been awake for five days.

The doctor was a fiftyish opera-loving queer who worked mainly as a gynecologist. We knew each other from the Horreya Café. He went there for the young boys, me for the watered-down beer. The doctor was a gentleman, unlike the bar's headwaiter, whom I once had to hit because he was groping me. After that it was established that I was not attracted to men.

Despite it all, the doctor and I became friends. This friendship was endlessly useful to me, as I could turn to him with all my health issues. If I had problems he would help me without charge. In one of my more lucid moments I recalled having had sex with at least ten Sudanese prostitutes without once using a condom. There, between the Horreya's fly-ridden tables, the doctor took a blood sample and personally delivered it to the lab. He submitted it under his own name, lest the HIV test come back positive, which would have meant my deportation from the country.

So, in the end, I put myself in Dr. Asim's hands for my sleeplessness cure. He prescribed Xanax. He sternly instructed me to take no more than three pills at once. He told me to take them one hour before I lay down to sleep. And it worked. To sleep four or five hours was a huge improvement after 160 hours awake. I felt like I was in heaven.

I was able to sleep normally for about a month, and then my money began to run out. Hearing that the Gaza border crossing had allegedly been opened by the Egyptian army was all it took for me to abandon Cairo and make my way toward the border. My editors were most eagerly awaiting my articles on the Egyptian-Palestinian conflict.

I found a Palestinian cabbie and set off for Arish.

Five hours later, we arrived.

For a small fortune I procured three bottles of beer from the town's only four-star hotel bar, then checked into the relatively affordable Sinai Star Motel. I planned on getting to bed early, so I took the prescribed three tablets and washed them down with beer. My last memory was of going to the reception desk to ask for a wake-up call.

There were five beds in the infirmary. The walls sparkled yellow from the potassium nitrate; a fan churned the smell of decay around the room. A thirtyish, unshaven man lay in the bed next to me, his leg in a cast up to his thigh.

"Hey foreigner, got a cigarette?" he asked in a raspy voice.

"Yep," I said, and reflexively reached down to my pocket. The hospital's considerate staff, however, had undressed me while I was unconscious; aside from the standard issue hospital pajamas, I had nothing on. With the movement I'd almost pulled the drip from my hand. I let my head fall back on the pillow and then looked around. By the door stood a large wardrobe. I guessed that my stuff was in it. With my left hand I carefully peeled the adhesive tape from my vein and pulled the IV from my hand, then turned on my side and put my foot on the ground. Standing was difficult, and I felt horribly faint, but I gathered my strength and stumbled across the room.

"It's not so urgent, foreigner," said the Arab.

"I want a smoke as well."

I'd guessed right: in the wardrobe I found my backpack and clothing. I reached into my pants pocket and pulled out the cigarettes and lighter, then staggered over to my neighbor's bed. I offered the pack to him, then put one in my mouth.

"It's OK if we smoke inside?"

"This is Egypt. We smoke everywhere. Now give me a light."

I lit his cigarette and then my own. He smoked, but didn't take his gaze from me for a moment.

"I don't think I have ever seen such a pale person in all my life," he finally said, tapping the ash from his cigarette onto the floor. "What are you doing here?"

"I'm a reporter. I want to go to Gaza."

"Through the tunnels?"

"No. The army said the border is open."

"The border's closed. You can only cross by tunnel."

"That's not what they told me in Cairo."

"They lied. They always lie."

We fell silent for a bit as we smoked.

"What's your name?"

"Daniel Marosh. I'm Hungarian."

"I am Abdelsabur ibn Abdelkader ibn Abdelmoati abu Al Asal."

"Pretty long name."

"Call me Abed," he said, then flicked the butt out the open window.

The doctor told me we'd need to wait and see if I had a concussion, so I would have to stay in the hospital for a few days. There was no cafeteria in the building, and patients had to take care of their own meals, though this was easily solved by the nearby food stands. I think it was because he kept asking me for various favors—things he couldn't do on account of his condition—such as bringing him food, that I became fast friends with the Bedouin.

Abed came from the Sawarka tribe. His son was a sheikh, and knew everything that was going on in the borderlands. Like everybody else in the tribe, Abed earned his living from the arms trade and people smuggling. He made no secret of this. His father ran fifteen tunnels in Rafah; and, though still young, Abed had two boys of his own. He quickly suggested that I make the crossing into the Gaza Strip through a tunnel—an offer I politely declined. I couldn't risk getting kicked out of the country.

After that, we talked about whatever came to mind. He told me about his tribe, and how many of his family members, his brothers, were in prison without trial; about how he and others had attacked a police building during the revolution and freed them. He told me about the fragile peace forged between the tribes and about blood feuds—about how, by law, he was responsible not only for himself but also for every member of the tribe.

Our conversation was interrupted only when the doctor came by, but that didn't happen too often. The doctor saw me just four times in my four days at the hospital. On his visits he would ask me to lie back in my bed and follow his pen with my eyes. He wrote the results in a white notebook and hummed with satisfaction.

Abed and I really talked about everything—that is, everything besides how we had each landed in the hospital. Abed avoided the topic, and I was mostly concerned with how I could best get some sleep. Luckily I'd been given some pills by the doctor to take before bed. My daily four hours were assured.

Despite this, the nights were still unspeakably long. The cement tower blocks, like the one we were in, slowly disgorged the heat that they had absorbed over the course of the day. Even with the fan running, the stiflingly humid air of the room seemed almost still.

It was on one of those nights when Abed told me about how he broke his leg. We were already in bed, but neither of us could sleep. The light from a streetlamp was shining in through an open window, so we could see still each other clearly. Unable to find a comfortable position, Abed stirred restlessly in bed.

"You know how this happened?" he asked, finally turning toward me and tapping on his cast. "I'll tell you, but you have to promise not to laugh."

"I promise."

"The thing is, I have this Chinese pistol. . . ."

"Really?"

"Really. It's a fine pistol, but you always have to keep it in good repair and well-oiled because of the sand."

"Don't tell me that . . ."

"Yes, I pulled the trigger. I didn't think that there was still a bullet in the barrel. Don't you dare laugh!"

"You were lucky."

"The doctor said God was merciful with me. The round went straight through my leg. I didn't even need surgery or anything."

"You really *were* lucky."

"God loves me."

We went quiet. Once again it was Abed who broke the silence.

"And you, *Abu Magari*"—this meant "Hungarian father"—"how did you come to be here?"

"I can't sleep."

"People don't usually go to the hospital for that."

"I haven't been able to sleep for three months."

"And before these three months, how could you sleep?"

"I was another person."

"And what happened?"

"My wife abandoned me and took our child."

"She cheated?"

"I believe so. Many times."

"And what did you do?"

"I don't know. That's probably why I can't sleep."

"No, I mean what did you do when you found out she cheated?"

"I came back to Africa."

"Why didn't you put a bullet in her head?" he asked with sincere outrage.

"That's not a custom with us."

"If you had shot her in the head, at least you could get some sleep."

Abed wouldn't let anybody visit because he was embarrassed that he had shot himself in the leg. On the fourth day, however, when it was time for him to be released, his brothers came.

That morning the doctor had told Abed that he could go, but the cast needed to stay on his leg for a few more weeks. I don't know if it was because we were together in the room, but the doctor also told me I could leave. There was just one problem with this: the bus that would take me to my hotel in Cairo wouldn't leave until evening.

It was around ten, and we were just picking over the remains of a late breakfast, when two teenagers in track suits stepped into the ward, sandals on their dirty feet. They grinned as they went over to Abed's bed and greeted him. They spoke in the Bedouin dialect, so I didn't understand a word. They helped Abed up from the bed, pressed a crutch into his hand, and then, at the man's order, began to pack his stuff from the wardrobe.

Abed changed into his brown jellabiya, then looked over at me.

"Get ready, Abu Magari, because you are coming with us," he said with a smile.

"Why?" I asked, though I reflected that the question should really be, *Why not?* For three months it had been my policy to strike the word "no" from my vocabulary.

"Does it really matter where you can't sleep?" Abed asked.

"When it comes down to it, not so much."

"So get your stuff together. Come with me. We'll have a good meal and I'll show you the desert." The two teenagers quickly picked up on the situation. The boys each shook my hand and introduced themselves. They were called Muhammad and Ahmed. I quickly packed my stuff, threw my backpack over my shoulder, and headed out with them.

It took us a while to make our way down the hospital steps, because of Abed's cast. Waiting in front of the building was a white Mitsubishi pickup. One boy flipped open the vehicle's tail-gate, jumped in, and helped Abed up, then moved into the front seat and started the ignition.

"Now what is it, Abu Magari, are you waiting for night to fall?" yelled the grinning Abed. I climbed in next to him. "Move the rifles if you need more space."

Three weather-beaten AK-47s lay next to where Abed sat. I pushed them aside, took a place next to the Bedouin, and hung on. With his palm, Abed hit the side of the vehicle. The back wheels churned up dust and in no time we were on the road to Sheikh Zuweid.

Abed the Bedouin lived in a large cement house with his family. Next to the house stood a white tent, which was always full of the men of the Sawarka tribe. Although Abed's father lived a few miles away, he walked over every day so he could discuss business affairs with the tribal elders. They had much to talk about: for instance, they couldn't make sense of the civil law book and didn't understand why it would be a criminal matter if they sold arms to their Muslim brothers in the Gaza Strip—not a day went by without a dispute with the local authorities. And, at the market, they bickered with other tribes over customers.

The men received me with a great show of affection after Abed explained the situation. Later that same day the two boys took me to show me the tunnels in Rafah. They proudly chattered in the front seat as we drove past the collapsing, sagging houses on the dirt road, beneath which ran the tunnels.

By the time we'd returned from Rafah, the men were getting ready for dinner. Everything had been set out in the tent for twenty people.

We ate together, in Bedouin fashion: without utensils, and using the right hand to scoop up the food, then washing the hand clean in a common bowl once finished.

After the meal, the lively gathering continued in the tent; the conversation lasted until eleven. Many of them joked that they would take a Hungarian woman as a second wife no matter what the cost. After midnight, however, the men began to trickle home.

"I'll show you your room," said Abed, when it was just us two. "You are a good person, Abu Magari, and I am glad you are here. Stay for as long as you want; you are always welcome as my guest."

"Thank you."

The Bedouin led the way to my floor. In the room was a single bed that Abed's wife had made up with a fresh sheet.

"Tomorrow we'll go shooting," he said. Then, with his crutch under his arm, he shuffled away.

I lay in bed for two hours, trying to sleep. I closed my eyes and waited for a dream to arrive. But none came.

At three I got out of bed and opened my backpack to look for my medicine case. When I found it, I spilled the entire contents on the floor, in the hope that I might find a few stray Xanax pills, because in the hospital they had confiscated the lot of them. There were none to be found.

Right then I caught sight of an old book under the bed. It was in German, published in 1936, written by one Hans Alexander Winkler, entitled *Die reitenden Geister der Toten*. A handwritten dedication on the title page, in black ink, read: *"Für Abd el Radi mit Liebe. Hans Alexander, Cairo, 1938."*

To distract myself from my torment, I began to read. It was an anthropological study about a certain man named Abd el Radi, who was a ghost rider. People like him were called ghost riders because allegedly they could mount the spirit of a dead person, who could then communicate with the living through them. The book dealt at length with how the *Bakhit*, or spirit, bound people with or released them from curses, tying such knots and untying them, and how it conjured up vengeful fire spirits from ash and blood.

By six the next morning I had finished the book. My nerves were on fire. *Devil take me*, I thought. And that didn't seem like a bad idea.

The machine gun crackled in my hands. In the distance, clouds of sand shot up far from the soda bottles we had set out as targets.

"Try again," said Abed. "Use your shoulder to better brace the gun." I did as he said and fired again. This time the sand cloud rose closer to the bottles.

We were by Mount Halal, somewhere in the middle of the desert. The sun was blazing; I was faint with sleeplessness.

"You can't concentrate."

He took the gun from my hand. The wood stock of the Czech Kalashnikov gleamed in the sun.

"Well, no," I said and wiped my brow. Squinting, I watched how the Bedouin fumbled with his bad leg to position himself for the shot. He took a long time to aim, and then pulled the trigger.

His shot didn't find the target either. He swore loudly, and then secured the gun.

"It seems I can't either," he said with a grin. "Now, come, Abu Magari, let's go back to the city and have something to eat."

We walked back to the truck. Unperturbed, Abed drove with his bad leg, though for this he needed to push the seat all the way back. He floored it past the villages, and slowed the vehicle only when we drove past the ruins of an Israeli airport, where, in the distance there appeared the metal fence and palm trees that lined the base of the international peacekeeping force.

"I found this last night," I said to Abed, pulling the book from my pants pocket and placing it on the table. We were sitting in a small restaurant in Arish, eating roast chicken. "It's dedicated," I pointed out.

"Yes. My grandfather's younger brother was Abd el Radi. Where did you find it?"

"Under the bed."

"My father must have left it there when he stayed with us."

"He knows German?"

"No."

"Then why did he have it?"

"There are pictures in it. Sometimes he'd look at them. We don't have many pictures of my grandfather and Abd el Radi."

I listened as I pushed rice around with my fork.

"I'd like to go see a ghost rider," I said.

"For what?" asked Abed. "Because of your wife, right?"

I nodded.

"You should have shot her and been done with it."

"But I didn't."

"Age-old mistake."

We went quiet. Abed picked his teeth with a bone, and then pointed to the book.

"That was a long time ago. Since then things have changed. There aren't many ghost riders left. Let's drive a little then watch some TV. Or we could find somebody with an Internet connection. For the other stuff, you need to be a Bedouin."

"It was just an idea."

"A bad idea."

We left it like that and went back to the house. Abed had to take care of some things in the afternoon; I left him to it and wrote an article about the Egypt-Israeli border, the tunnels that ran under Rafah, and the Bedouins who ran them.

Abed returned around sunset. After eating dinner with the men, my host introduced me to his two small sons.

Both boys were five. The Bedouin introduced me like I was a film star, after which the boys hung on me and pulled at my hair. They simply couldn't believe I had blonde hair.

I began to feel increasingly tense, however, as bedtime neared. The melting of days into each other, one of the first symptoms of chronic insomnia, is still bearable, especially in company. The hell begins when you find yourself alone in the night.

By morning my eyes were totally bloodshot. When Abed found me I was sitting on the floor, so I could watch the sun rise from between the hills of the desert.

"OK," he said, shaking his head. "I'll take you to a ghost rider."

We left the house at noon. Abed had to make several calls to figure out where a ghost rider lived who would be willing to see us. No sooner did he find one than we were off. The desert was blindingly white; before our eyes the ultramarine sky melted into the horizon.

We had been driving for an hour before Abed spoke.

"You know you will have to pay him."

"I do. Do you know the man?"

"No. My nephew told me how to find him. He's called Ahmed Ustazi."

"OK."

"What is it you want?"

"To drive away the devil."

"Anything more concrete?"

"I don't think so."

"We'll see what he recommends."

We let it drop. A few minutes later a row of palm huts appeared in the distance. When we pulled up, all the village's children were standing along the road, gaping at the car. Abed slowed to a stop and greeted them.

"Peace be upon you. Where can we find Ahmed Ustazi's tent?"

The kids scattered at the mention of the ghost rider's name. We started off toward the center of the village.

"Are you sure we're in the right place?" I asked Abed.

"I'm sure."

We were at the outer huts, when we noticed an old woman.

Abed, leaning his crutch up against a hut, asked her where the ghost rider lived; she pointed to the distance. A brown tent stood almost half a mile away.

As we approached the tent, my nose caught the smell of carrion. Abed went into the tent first; I followed. For a few minutes I couldn't see anything in the dimly lit space, then, as my eyes adjusted, I was able make out the interior.

From the tent's ceiling the rotting carcasses of kestrels, their wings spread wide, hung on plastic cords, flies buzzing around them.

Under the kestrels stood a beat-up writing table covered with bowls and trash. A forty-something man in a jellabiya sat in front of the table in a woven chair. His face was grubby, and he was missing an eye.

"Peace be upon you," he said. That was the most I understood of his Bedouin dialect. We approached the table, then Abed explained the situation, waving his hands for emphasis. The man turned toward me and said something I couldn't understand.

"He said he doesn't know a curse that can drive away the devil," Abed translated, then added, "But he does know one to use if you can't rest, if you never feel satisfied and can't love anybody, not even yourself."

"That will work," I said. Right then, I felt that the tent was dissolving, me along with it. I teetered, and then reached into my pocket, where I kept a bottle. I took a few swigs of the lukewarm mineral water.

Abed looked at me with worry. Again, the ghost rider spoke.

"He said that this would be the strongest knot."

"OK."

"You will need something of your wife's. Do you have anything from her?"

"A boy," I said, and leaned on the table for support. Abed translated. The ghost rider picked up a rusty scalpel from the table. Before I had time to realize it, he'd made a two-inch-long cut on my hand. It was deep, and blood began to immediately flow from the wound. From under the trash on the table, he produced a blue plastic dish. He held my hand over the dish, so my cut could drip into it. He scattered bird feathers and sand in the blood, then began to chant.

Because of my sleeplessness, the tent again began to spin, only that this time I didn't lose my balance. I gazed at the ghost rider, who was bending over my hand, mumbling something; I watched my blood, how it rhythmically dripped into the plastic dish.

A cell phone sounded. It started quietly, but became increasingly loud, until the preinstalled Nokia ringtone filled the tent. The ghost rider stood upright, then reached into the pocket of his jellabiya, took out the phone, and began to talk. He spoke in a Cairo accent, which I understood perfectly. The topic of conversation was a car. I gathered that he was selling it and a potential buyer was on the line. Abed and I looked at each other questioningly, but the ghost rider wasn't in the least bit embarrassed.

The man described the car's attributes at length: the tires and condition of the rims, as well as the battery, which he had changed just a few weeks ago. When he finished the conversation he carefully put the phone back in his pocket, looked at me and my bleeding hand, and said only this:

"We're alright."

Abed translated, though it wasn't necessary. This, I already understood. I also well understood the next sentence:

"That will be a hundred dollars."

I reached into the pocket of my leather jacket, took out my last hundred-dollar bill, and pressed it into the man's hand. I then left the tent. Abed followed.

I took my scarf from my neck and wrapped it around my hand, then sat holding it in the car.

We pulled away quickly, soon leaving the village behind. We gazed at the desert that rushed past and the hills in the distance.

For a while we sat in silence, then the Bedouin said, "You know, you can still shoot her." We then agreed that although the wound on my hand wasn't too serious, it would be a good idea if we stopped in Arish to pick up some disinfectant.

The Dead Ride Fast

Wie flog, was rund der Mond beschien,
Wie flog es in die Ferne!
Wie flogen oben überhin
Der Himmel und die Sterne! -
"Graut Liebchen auch? . . . Der Mond scheint hell!
Hurra! Die Toten reiten schnell! –
Graut Liebchen auch vor Toten?"
"O weh! laß ruhn die Toten!"

How flew to the right, how flew to the left,
Trees, mountains in the race!
How to the left, and the right and the left,
Flew town and marketplace!
"What ails my love? the moon shines bright:
Bravely the dead men ride thro' the night.
Is my love afraid of the quiet dead?"
"Ah! let them alone in their dusty bed!"
                    —Gottfried August Bürger, "Lenore"*

* Translated from the German by Gabriel Charles Rosetti

She wrote to say she wasn't going to let me see the child. I read the email through once more, then thought it would be a good time to put on my jacket and go out into the fighting on the street. It would be better than writing back and spending the rest of the night staring into the monitor, waiting for a response. I wasn't in the mood to tell her for the thousandth time not to blackmail me with my own child.

Out on the street they were fighting for peace. Cairo was burning. The demonstrators attacked the Interior Ministry with sticks and stones. The police had begun firing into the crowds. Typically it pleases me when there is fighting, as it gives me work with which to occupy myself.

I'd seen four wars in the year that passed since she took the child. I had no idea how much morphine I would consume, how many barroom brawls and dogfights I'd see, how many Sudanese whores I would fuck in backstreet brothels before the madness and rage would be driven from me. But what was left was aimlessness; I didn't know how to move forward. If I didn't keep myself occupied, I'd just sit there gazing at my navel for days or even weeks. On that night, as on many nights, I preferred to put on my coat, check my camera, and grab a taxi.

The driver didn't want to take me to Tahrir Square, so I had to walk across Qasr al-Nil Bridge, where a large crowd had gathered, gaping dumbfounded at the oily black smoke rising from the city center. An armored personnel carrier was in flames by the entrance to the square. Wide red stains darkened the cement, but the bodies were nowhere to be seen. The demonstrators must have taken them to a nearby mosque. I imagined they'd been laid out on the mosque's synthetic green prayer carpets and wrapped in white blankets, which the blood would slowly seep through. I had seen this before, at the outbreak of the uprising. The bodies began to reek within an hour, and the blood flowed from them as though they were still living.

The shards of a broken windshield crunched under my shoes as I got closer to the fire. I took a picture of a young hooded man. He was shouting "Murderers, murderers!" at the black-clad riot police, spittle flying from his mouth.

The crowd that had assembled by the square's entrance was throwing rocks at the riot police. I snapped five or so pictures before the demonstrators surged. Smoke grenades sliced through the air above, white trails in their wake. The police line broke, and eight men stepped forward and began to fire with shotguns. Those who took the shots in the front line fell. From the rear rows people ran clutching their faces, blood running between their fingers. From twenty meters, a shotgun blast is no longer lethal, but it can still take out an eye. Everybody began to flee. I ran with the crowd all the way to the bridge.

The escape didn't last long—just until we were out of the guns' range. The police closed off their formation, then retreated to the front of Qasr al-Ayni Street. I had accidentally hit somebody with a camera lens during the surge, and was forced to stop and check that the glass hadn't shifted; only afterward did I start heading back with the demonstrators, who were again throwing stones. I shot a series of two young boys, Molotov cocktails in their hands, charging toward the police.

Right then I saw Sahra Gamal. She was kneeling at Mohamed Mahmoud Street, a Nikon D5 in her hand. We knew each other— she'd been there during the recent conflicts in Libya and Gaza; she was a brave woman, one of the bravest I'd known. Sahra, who had duel German and Egyptian citizenship, worked for *Der Spiegel*. She never turned down an assignment, and had seen some of the fiercest action around. So it was no surprise to see her there on one knee, in a scarf, her breasts bound with cloth. For the first time, it struck me what a beautiful woman she was. I went and stood beside her.

"Let's get a drink after the next barrage," I said. Before she could answer, a fresh attack came and the fleeing crowd separated us. It had grown dark. The streetlights on Tahrir Square had been turned on. In front of the Mugamma building where volunteer doctors were assembling tents, the wounded lay moaning on the muddy, blood-caked mats; you could see their breath in the air. The cold came suddenly. The sun had almost completely disappeared from the horizon, and the temperature dropped to around five degrees. In many places across the square, fires blazed. On Mohamed Mahmoud Street there was still fighting, and the barricades had been set alight.

David Sanders, an American photojournalist, called to see where I was, and showed up later amid the fighting. We had worked alongside one another several times in the past. He was with Reuters, so we didn't step on each other's toes. It's good to have somebody around who knows you. In a worst-case scenario he can lie and deliver some wise dying words to your family, or embellish an otherwise pointless death with some heroic details.

We emerged from Mohamed Mahmoud Street, our faces burning from tear gas and our shoes making a wet, smacking sound against the pavement from the mixture of oil and mud. My leather jacket was speckled with buckshot holes, and Sanders's old Soviet coat hadn't fared much better. I took my gas mask from my face, sat on a bench, and lit a cigarette. Sanders—who was tall, black-haired, and Jewish—sat next to me, dropping his 5D in his lap. Dirt outlined the place where his mask had been.

"It's getting dark," he said.

"Yeah, we're fucked for more pictures."

"Right. How many did you get?"

He took the cigarette from my hand and had a drag. I looked at the indicator.

"Three hundred and forty-eight."

"I got around that many as well. It's enough."

"My face is burning."

"So is mine. Let's grab a drink."

"Where?"

"Well, I'm not about to cross over to Zamalek. So here at the Lotus."

"Okay, let's go."

I felt dizzy from the gas and my limbs were heavy. Sanders was also out of it; we could barely drag ourselves along. The Lotus stood at the head of Talaat Harb Street. It was one of the few places that held a license to sell alcohol. Nobody ever actually stayed there; the mattresses had bedbugs, the sheets were grimy, and there was never any hot water.

To get to the bar, you had to ring a bell on the wall, signaling the headwaiter, who would send the elevator down. Even as we ascended we could hear the thrum from the street. As soon as we stepped from the elevator, our faces were hit with cigarette smoke. Every table was crowded with journalists; practically the entire international media was there. Alcohol hinders the absorption of tear gas into the bloodstream, and it eases the poison's effects. Everybody there was guzzling drink after drink.

I peeled myself from my equipment and sat at the bar.

"What will the gentlemen be having?" the headwaiter asked.

"*Itnēn* Auld Stag, *min fadlik*."

He nodded, grabbed two dusty water glasses from the shelf, rinsed them out, then took some ice from a bucket.

"Single or double?" he asked, bottle in hand.

"Double," we said simultaneously.

He poured and we each downed ours in a gulp.

"Another?"

I nodded yes. I was drinking on an empty stomach; I could feel the alcohol run up my spine.

"What's the score?" asked Sanders and staggered over to the TV, which was showing Mohamed Mahmoud Street. In the dark only the flaming barricades and the flashes from the police rifles could be seen. Al Jazeera was broadcasting live from one of the apartments on the square.

"Thirteen dead, more than three hundred wounded," said the headwaiter, placing the next round in front of us. "Though the Ministry of Health hasn't confirmed that yet."

"Well, at least it wasn't us," said Sanders.

We drank to the fact that we had gotten through the day alive, that we were OK. We were still alive to file one more story, to spend another day in a foreign country with foreign inhabitants, in the middle of a foreign conflict.

"I'm going to wash my face," I said and headed toward the restroom on the floor below; a grimy rug covered the steps that led there. Halfway down I came face to face with Sahra Gamal. She had already taken off her scarf, her black hair falling to her shoulders. Her face was damp with water.

"Now, can I invite you for a drink?" I said.

"I'd rather just go to my place."

She took my hand, climbed to one step above me, and kissed my lips. I could smell the tear gas on her skin. We went back to the bar together to get my stuff. Sanders was already stupidly drunk. He looked at me and in a gurgling voice said, "Watch out. That one's crazy."

Sahra lived in a three-room apartment in Heliopolis. "Do it so it hurts," she said as we undressed. We didn't shower; we simply stripped ourselves of our clothing and fell all over each other on her Ikea bed. Her eyes flashed when I wrapped my hands around her neck. I pinned her down on the bed and entered her.

Afterward we lay wordlessly next to each other.

I was staring at a picture on the wall, a 2009 World Press Photo winner, showing a Palestinian woman carrying the body of a dead child. The shot was taken with a 55 mm lens, the photographer standing opposite her.

"Did you take that?" I asked, indicating the picture. Her neck was still red from my grasp.

"Yes," she said and took hold of my outstretched hand. She was staring at the ring on my finger.

"Are you married?" she asked.

"No."

"Then why the ring? You don't have to lie."

"It's not a lie. I'm not married."

"Then why the ring?"

"It's stuck to my finger. I can't take it off anymore. I was married, though."

"What happened?"

"She thought I was getting in the way of her career as a writer."

"When was this?"

"Last year. And she took our child."

"And? Did you love her?"

"Yes."

"Doesn't it bother you to wear the ring, then?"

"It does; I just can't take it off."

She looked at the ring on my finger for a while, then said, "Why don't you cut it off?"

"Because I like my finger."

We fell silent again. I wasn't in the mood to tell her that the mother of my child had slept with my enemies at every opportunity, that she seemed to take great joy in my destruction. I didn't want to tell her how my heart had stopped in Arish from all the tranquilizers I'd taken, or how once I hadn't slept for a week, 165 hours, to be exact. I didn't want her to know that my ex was blackmailing me with parental visitations, and how, in the end, you could do anything to another person with no consequences. It had nothing to do with her.

"And, you, what's your story?" I asked. It occurred to me that anybody over the age of thirty must have one. "Just screwing around?"

"Mine died in Iraq."

"I'm sorry."

"Don't be. He went and got himself shot."

"Was he in the press?"

"Yes."

"Did you love him?"

"I was pregnant when he died."

"I'm sorry."

"You needn't be. I got rid of it."

"Why?"

"Because you don't deliver babies to dead people."

She got up and went to the bathroom. I could hear her turn on the shower. I looked at my watch; it was 1 AM. I rose from the bed and began to dress.

I found her in the hall, wrapped in a white towel.

"If you want to sleep here, I can make up the couch."

"Just a blanket is fine. Thanks."

She stepped over to a closet, took out a light blue blanket, and put it into my hands.

"Lock the door on your way out when you leave."

In the shower, I used her lavender body gel, and then went to bed. I couldn't sleep, however. I kept looking at the photos on the wall in the dim light of the room. They were all hers, and they all took place in the heat of battle. She had been to every one of those places in the last seven years, and in each place she had been on the front line of an armed conflict. It suddenly came to me that, if indications were true, other people also had shitty lives.

I checked my phone. My editor needed the pictures from the night before. I sent him an email and headed out.

Glass from the smashed storefront windows crunched under my feet along Talat Harb Street. I felt queasy. I thought I might walk down Mohamed Mahmoud Street, snap a few shots of the burning barricades, and then, while I was there, go have a drink. Sanders was already in Alexandria shooting the ruckus there, so I was quite alone.

A huge crowd had already gathered on Tahrir Square. A bearded man in a robe stood at the square's opening, toweling off his face.

"What's happening?" I asked.

"We are keeping them busy so they can't enter the square."

"How many are injured?"

"I don't know, but the dead are in the Omar Makram Mosque. They are there, and there are more than a few."

"Thanks."

"Allah Karim."

The air was thick with tear gas and the smoke from burning trash. I took my camera from its case, set it to the night photography mode, and headed down Mohamed Mahmoud Street. The Central Security Forces had cut the power to the entire district. On both sides of the street the trash bins and barricades were ablaze; the demonstrators had lit them to keep the tear gas attacks at bay and to see movement in the night.

An ambulance tried to cut through the heaving crowd, but the sirens couldn't be heard above the sounds of shotguns and fighting.

On the nearby streets the fighting continued. I saw lit Molotov cocktails in the hands of the surging crowd, but there wasn't enough light to get photos of them. A tear gas grenade cut through the air, emitting a thick white wake of smoke, and landed a few yards from where I was standing. I put my gas mask on. It wasn't the best equipment; I had bought it for twenty-five dollars from a street vendor. It was meant for industrial use, not for a tear gas attack. Still, it worked.

A second grenade hit the ground, bounced along the cement, and began to smoke. Another followed, then a fourth. A panicked escape ensued. I clutched my camera and began to shoot, flattening myself against the wall so I wouldn't get carried along with the crowd.

I didn't hear the bang of the rifle, didn't see the barrel flash; I just felt the blow. My head hit the cement. The gas mask was knocked off, and my lungs filled. I was suddenly overcome with calm, the likes of which I hadn't felt since my divorce. As the world around me went dark, the thought entered my mind that everything had come to an end. It had come to an end on a moonless Middle Eastern night, doing away with those questions of who I was and what I was doing here; doing away with the senseless quest for money, and that money's even more senseless spending.

I have no idea how long I was out. When I came to, I felt hands upon me.

"He is wearing a vest," said somebody in Arabic.

I opened my eyes. Sahra Gamal was standing over me with two of the demonstrators.

"You OK?" she asked.

"Yes," I said. It hurt to speak.

"You were shot. Lucky thing you had a vest on."

"Yes," I said, and sat up. My side hurt terribly, and blood was dripping from my forehead into my eye.

"Is there somebody we should contact?"

"No, nobody."

"Your paper?"

"I'm freelance."

"Can you stand?"

"I think so."

I used Sahra to hold me up as I hobbled all the way to Qasr al-Nil Bridge. From there we got a taxi.

"Here, take this," she said once we were in the apartment.

"What is it?"

"A painkiller."

I swallowed the pill. We were standing in the bedroom again. Sahra unbuttoned my shirt, put her hand against my black Kevlar vest, and then ran her fingers all along my side.

"They shot you here."

"Yes."

Her hand found the Velcro, then ripped it loose and took the vest off me. The whole spectrum of the rainbow could be seen on my side.

"Does it hurt when you inhale?"

"Yes."

"You probably broke a rib. Lean back."

I leaned back. She took off my boots, my socks, then unbuttoned my belt and pulled my pants off. After she finished, she also began to undress, and then reclined next to me on the bed. Now, for the first time, I took in her entire body. I'd been with lots of women since my divorce, but I never examined the whole of their naked bodies. I simply wasn't interested. I only wanted them to satisfy my needs, nothing more. I wouldn't have used them if I had come to know their bodies' flaws. A flaw personalized them.

Sahra's body was marred by scar tissue and cuts, but it was still beautiful. I gazed at her brown skin for a while, the little black nipples. On the inner part of her right hand was tattooed in black letters, *Die Toten Reiten Schnell*. It was a new tattoo; it couldn't have been more than a year old, as there was no fading.

"What does it mean?" I asked, running a finger over it.

"To ride fast like the dead. It's German."

"I understand that, but why did you have it inked there?"

"To remind myself."

"Of what?"

"That the dead don't hold back anything, because the worst has already happened to them. Their lives were taken."

"And you think you are dead?"

"I don't think I lived past what happened to me. I have no life outside my work, no purpose, no desire. I am like the dead. With just a memory of who I was."

"That's bullshit."

"No, it's not. I know you know what I'm talking about. You also died; I saw it in your eyes."

"We've both done some pretty lively things. Together, for example."

"It's a way to pass the time."

"You want to die?"

"No. It just doesn't matter if I die. Or you, for that matter. You don't have a family you need to go home to, or even a wife anymore. You don't have anything. Just your camera and your work. You're already dead; you just haven't realized it yet."

"I'm tired," I said.

"From the pill."

"From everything. Can I sleep here?"

"Yes."

"I snore when I dream."

"I cry."

"No problem," I said, and took her in my arms.

I woke up from the ache in my side. Sahra was still asleep. She was tucked in up to the neck; you could see only her hair on the pillow. The clock read 8 AM. I climbed from the bed, collected my clothing from the floor, and started toward the bathroom. I stopped in front of the foyer mirror and had a look at my side: it was black, but in happier news, the wound on my head didn't appear too bad and I didn't feel faint. I most likely hadn't gotten a concussion.

I used Sahra's shower gel as I washed. By the time I finished, she had woken and was standing undressed in the kitchen.

"Want a coffee?"

"Sure."

"How's your side?"

"It hurts."

"You should go to a doctor."

"Not a chance. There's a revolution on."

She smiled and placed a mug of coffee in front of me, then turned. She stepped up to the fridge, took out the butter, and with her back still to me, began to spread some on a slice of bread. I stared, all the while thinking that this was a preposterously beautiful woman.

"Look, you know we can meet like normal people do sometime," I said. "For example, we could go to a restaurant. We could eat like normal people, and I could try to get you drunk enough to sleep with me."

"I'll gladly sleep with you again. No need for fireworks."

"You're not getting it. Can't we go somewhere, anywhere, and do something like regular people?"

"That's daft. There's no point. There is no point in romance."

"I'm still alive. You should give it a try."

She turned on the TV. The Al Jazeera newscaster's British-accented voice filled the kitchen. It was streaming from the city center, showing violent fighting everywhere.

"Let's think about getting to work," said Sahra. "Get your stuff together."

They had put the injured on prayer rugs. In the mosque's haze, the demonstrators were placing lamps between the rows of bodies. The doctors circulated among them like angels in white coats. They bent down, checked pulses, examined wounds, and gave injections. But the real work took place in a space cordoned off by curtains: that's where the serious cases were taken. Burn victims and those with shattered bones howled from pain, drowning out the sound of the Koran recitation coming from a speaker, whose voice at times rose loud enough to accompany the sound of the sick, giving the holy text an altogether more moving recitation. I photographed the wounded. I felt heavily medicated, but at least my side didn't hurt.

I didn't see Sahra for the next three days. I tried to drive her from my thoughts and concentrate on work instead. After work I dutifully went home and uploaded my photos. By night I surfed the Web. I did a search for her there but found only a single photo. In the picture she was locked in an embrace with a man somewhere that looked like the Congo. Both were smiling at the camera. It dawned on me that that was what she was like before.

It's possible she is right, I thought.

I was shooting a quick series while lying on the ground when my cell phone rang. It was Sanders.

"I heard you were shot, man."

"You heard right."

"But you're okay?"

"Peachy."

"Listen, remember that freaky German chick?"

"Yeah."

"Well she's been looking for you. I gave her your number. I hope that's not a problem."

"No."

"Did you bang her?"

"Yeah."

"Good work. We'll drink to it later. I'll be gone for a couple of days. So when I come back from Port Said."

"OK."

I put the phone away. I checked my photos, and then left the mosque.

Back home, I was sitting on the roof, uploading photos to the Internet. The FTP server was bloody slow, so I passed the time playing music and smoking.

At first I didn't hear the sound of the phone over the speakers. It must have been ringing for minutes before I picked it up.

"It's Sahra," came the voice over the line.

"Yes?"

"I just wanted to ask whether you have a 50 mm lens."

"Yeah, I've got one."

"Can I borrow it?"

"Of course. Where should we meet?"

"The restaurant at the Hilton."

"Right. What time?"

"Nine. Just don't be late; I want to eat too. I'll come from work, as I need a few nighttime pictures."

"OK. Anything else?"

"Yes. Take that ring off."

"Will do."

I had grown a serious beard since the turbulence broke out; I couldn't be bothered to shave, and there was nobody to tell me it irritated them. I gazed at myself for a while in the mirror before turning on the warm water and soaping up my face. I noticed the ring on my finger as I shaved off the first swath of lather. I gave it a pull. Indeed, it was still stuck tight. I picked up the soap again and began rubbing my finger. I grabbed the ring and began to tug, but it wouldn't come off. I had to go to the kitchen for a knife, and used that to get some soap between the skin and the gold—only after this did it slip from my finger, leaving a green stain in its place.

The Ramses Hilton was the most expensive hotel in town, and I couldn't really afford it. Still, I took a taxi from Dokki all the way to the 6th October Bridge. I tried to pay the driver extra money to take me all the way, but he was afraid of the demonstrators. I would have to walk, though in this neighborhood there was still no fighting. Both Tahrir Square and Mohamed Mahmoud Street were cordoned off.

There weren't any bellboys by the entrance due to the tear gas. Other than that, the hotel continued its business undisturbed. The guests here were primarily parachute journalists. They all occupied the rooms facing the square. With a good lens and use of the hotel's stable Internet connection, they could read from cue cards and broadcast live without ever having to go down into the fray.

From the tinted top-floor windows I could see the entire city on both sides of the Nile. Downtown was dark; from the twenty-fourth floor the burning barricades down on the street appeared like small dots of light, though the sound didn't reach that high.

The restaurant was totally empty. I took a table by the window and looked at my watch: it was nine o'clock; I was right on time. The waiter brought me a menu.

"Dining alone tonight, sir?"

"No, I am waiting for somebody."

"Very good. Shall I bring you a drink?"

"A bottle of cabernet."

"Egyptian?"

"Please."

Omar Khayyam was the only cabernet sauvignon in the country, and I knew I would pay a minimum of 200 Egyptian pounds for it at hotel prices. The waiter left. I reached into my jacket pocket, took out the lens Sahra had asked for, and placed it on the table. Out of boredom I scanned the Twitter feed on my cell and retweeted a government official's statement on the news about the country's economic affairs. The waiter came back with the wine, poured a little in my glass, and waited while I tasted it. I checked the time: Sahra was already twenty minutes late. I tipped back the wine and let him fill the glass. I continued to browse the news networks. The fighting around the country had intensified, at least according to Twitter. Young men had been bussed in and paid to attack the crowds with rocks and sticks.

I spent another twenty minutes like this. The waiter watched me from the bar. I refilled my glass, then looked up Sahra's number and dialed. It didn't ring. Instead a female voice informed me in Arabic that the phone was turned off, but they would send a text message alerting her that I had called. I tried several times more, but it didn't ring once. I drank another glass of wine. The waiter approached.

"Excuse me, sir, but theoretically the kitchen closes at ten. I can ask the chef to wait, however."

"No worries. I don't think she's coming."

"There is a revolution. It's possible she couldn't get into the city center."

"Perhaps."

"Would you care to dine?"

"No. Just the check please."

"As you wish."

I phoned one final time, again to no avail. I paid for the wine and rose from the table. I had to wait for the elevator; the fires were burning below, flaring up, then calming. Out on the street the wind was strong: my coat fluttered like a black flag as I crossed the bridge. On Twitter I read that the hired thugs were also attacking journalists; two Polish reporters and a German photographer had been killed. The next morning the Ministry of Health confirmed the story.

ALSO AVAILABLE FROM
NEW EUROPE BOOKS

"JOHN SHIRTING . . . STANDS IN THE GOOD COMPANY OF
IGNATIUS J. REILLY, CHAUNCEY GARDENER, AND FORREST GUMP."
—ANDREI CODRESCU

KEEPING BEDLAM AT BAY
IN THE PRAGUE CAFÉ
A NOVEL
M. HENDERSON ELLIS

978-0-9825781-8-6

"[G]enuine imagination and an
energetic wit."
—Publishers Weekly

"An ode to expatriate living, culture
clashes, and the heady days of early
1990s Europe, this novel is a manic,
wild ride."
—Booklist

"A hilarious hallucinatory satire, built on
shots of caffeine."
**—Amanda Stern,
author of
*The Long Haul***